FOUR

A DIVERGENT COLLECTION

"You'll be up all night with **DIVERGENT**, a brainy thrill-ride of a novel."

"The imaginative action and glimpses of a sprawling conspiracy are serious attention-grabbers, and the portrait of a shattered, derelict, overgrown, and abandoned Chicago is evocative as ever."

"Author Roth tells the riveting and complex story of a teenage girl forced to choose between her routinized, selfless family and the adventurous, unrestrained future she longs for.
A memorable, unpredictable journey from which it is nearly impossible to turn away."

"With brisk pacing and lavish flights of imagination, **DIVERGENT** clearly has thrills, but it also movingly explores a more common adolescent anxiety—the painful realization that coming into one's own sometimes means leaving family behind, both ideologically and physically."

"Nonstop, adrenaline-heavy action. Packed with stunning twists and devastating betrayals."

—BCCB

"**DIVERGENT** is really an extended metaphor about the trials of modern adolescence: constantly having to take tests that sort and rank you among your peers, facing separation from your family, agonizing about where you fit in, and deciding when (or whether) to reveal the ways you may diverge from the group."

—WALL STREET JOURNAL

"This gritty, paranoid world is built with careful details and intriguing scope. The plot clips along at an addictive pace, with steady jolts of brutal violence and swoony romance. Fans snared by the ratcheting suspense will be unable to resist speculating on their own factional allegiance."

—KIRKUS REVIEWS

"Roth knows how to write. The novel's love story, intricate plot, and unforgettable setting work in concert to deliver a novel that will rivet fans of the first book."

—PUBLISHERS WEEKLY

"In this addictive sequel to the acclaimed
DIVERGENT, a bleak postapocalyptic Chicago
collapses into all-out civil war.
Another spectacular cliff-hanger."

—KIRKUS REVIEWS

"**INSURGENT** explores several critical themes,
including the importance of family
and the crippling power of grief at its loss."

—SLJ

"Roth's plotting is intelligent and complex.
Dangers, suspicion, and tension lurk around every
corner, and the chemistry between Tris and Tobias
remains heart-poundingly real. . . . This final
installment will capture and hold attention until
the divisive final battle has been waged."

—PUBLISHERS WEEKLY

"The tragic conclusion, although shocking, is
thematically consistent; the bittersweet epilogue
offers a poignant hope."

—KIRKUS REVIEWS

Also by Veronica Roth

DIVERGENT

INSURGENT

ALLEGIANT

FOUR

A DIVERGENT COLLECTION

VERONICA ROTH

HarperCollins*Publishers*

First published in hardback in the US by HarperCollins Publishers Inc., in 2014
This edition published in hardback and paperback by HarperCollins Children's
Books, a division of HarperCollins Publishers Ltd, 77-85 Fulham Palace Road,
Hammersmith, London, W6 8JB in 2014

www.harpercollins.co.uk

HB ISBN: 978-0-00-756069-1
PB ISBN: 978-0-00-755014-2

Printed and bound in England by Clays Ltd, St Ives plc
Typography by Joel Tippie

14 15 16 17 18 10 9 8 7 6 5 4 3 2
❖
First Edition

To my readers, who are wise and brave.

CONTENTS

INTRODUCTION

I FIRST STARTED writing *Divergent* from the perspective of Tobias Eaton, a boy from Abnegation with peculiar tension with his father who longed for freedom from his faction. I reached a standstill at thirty pages because the narrator wasn't quite right for the story I wanted to tell; four years later, when I picked up the story again, I found the right character to drive it, this time a girl from Abnegation who wanted to find out what she was made of. But Tobias never disappeared—he entered the story as Four, Tris's instructor, friend, boyfriend, and equal. He has always been a character I was interested in exploring further because of the way he came alive for me every time he was on the page. He is powerful for me largely because of the way he continues to overcome adversity, even managing, on several occasions, to flourish in it.

The first three stories, "The Transfer," "The Initiate,"

and "The Son," take place before he ever meets Tris, following his path from Abnegation to Dauntless as he earns his own strength. In the last, "The Traitor," which overlaps chronologically with the middle of *Divergent*, he meets Tris. I wanted very much to include the moment when they meet, but unfortunately, it didn't fit into the story's timeline—you can find it instead at the back of this book.

The series follows Tris from the moment she seized control of her own life and identity; and with these stories, we can follow Four as he does the same. And the rest, as they say, is history.

—*Veronica Roth*

THE TRANSFER

I EMERGE FROM the simulation with a yell. My lip stings, and when I take my hand away from it, there is blood on my fingertips. I must have bitten it during the test.

The Dauntless woman administering my aptitude test—Tori, she said her name was—gives me a strange look as she pulls her black hair back and ties it in a knot. Her arms are marked up and down with ink, flames and rays of light and hawk wings.

"When you were in the simulation . . . were you aware that it wasn't real?" Tori says to me as she turns off the machine. She sounds and looks casual, but it's a studied casualness, learned from years of practice. I know it when I see it. I always do.

Suddenly I'm aware of my own heartbeat. This is what

my father said would happen. He told me that they would ask me if I was aware during the simulation, and he told me what to say when they did.

"No," I say. "If I was, do you think I would have chewed through my lip?"

Tori studies me for a few seconds, then bites down on the ring in her lip before she says, "Congratulations. Your result was textbook Abnegation."

I nod, but the word "Abnegation" feels like a noose wrapped around my throat.

"Aren't you pleased?" she says.

"My faction members will be."

"I didn't ask about them, I asked about you." Tori's mouth and eyes turn down at the corners like they bear little weights. Like she's sad about something. "This is a safe room. You can say whatever you want here."

I knew what my choices in the aptitude test would add up to before I arrived at school this morning. I chose food over a weapon. I threw myself in the path of the dog to save the little girl. I knew that after I made those choices, the test would end and I would receive Abnegation as a result. And I don't know that I would have made different choices if my father hadn't coached me, hadn't controlled every part of my aptitude test from afar. So what was I expecting? What faction did I want?

Any of them. Any of them but Abnegation.

"I'm pleased," I say firmly. I don't care what she says—this isn't a safe room. There are no safe rooms, no safe truths, no safe secrets to tell.

I can still feel the dog's teeth closing around my arm, tearing my skin. I nod to Tori and start toward the door, but just before I leave, her hand closes around my elbow.

"You're the one who has to live with your choice," she says. "Everyone else will get over it, move on, no matter what you decide. But you never will."

I open the door and walk out.

+++

I return to the cafeteria and sit down at the Abnegation table, among the people who barely know me. My father doesn't permit me to come to most community events. He claims that I'll cause a disruption, that I'll do something to hurt his reputation. I don't care. I'm happier in my room, in the silent house, than surrounded by the deferential, apologetic Abnegation.

The consequence of my constant absence, though, is that the other Abnegation are wary of me, convinced there's something wrong with me, that I'm ill or immoral or strange. Even those willing to nod at me in greeting don't quite meet my eyes.

I sit with my hands clenching my knees, watching the other tables, while the other students finish their aptitude tests. The Erudite table is covered in reading material, but they aren't all studying—they're just making a show of it, trading conversation instead of ideas, their eyes snapping back to the words every time they think someone's watching them. The Candor are talking loudly, as always. The Amity are laughing, smiling, pulling food from their pockets and passing it around. The Dauntless are raucous and loud, slung over the tables and chairs, leaning on one another and poking one another and teasing.

I wanted any other faction. Any other faction but mine, where everyone has already decided that I am not worth their attention.

Finally an Erudite woman enters the cafeteria and holds up a hand for silence. The Abnegation and Erudite quiet down right away, but it takes her shouting "Quiet!" for the Dauntless, Amity, and Candor to notice her.

"The aptitude tests are now finished," she says. "Remember that you are not permitted to discuss your results with *anyone*, not even your friends or family. The Choosing Ceremony will be tomorrow at the Hub. Plan to arrive at least ten minutes before it begins. You are dismissed."

Everyone rushes toward the doors except our table,

where we wait for everyone else to leave before we even get to our feet. I know the path my fellow Abnegation will take out of here, down the hallway and out the front doors to the bus stop. They could be there for over an hour letting other people get on in front of them. I don't think I can bear any more of this silence.

Instead of following them, I slip out a side door and into an alley next to the school. I've taken this route before, but usually I creep along slowly, not wanting to be seen or heard. Today all I want to do is run.

I sprint to the end of the alley and into the empty street, leaping over a sinkhole in the pavement. My loose Abnegation jacket snaps in the wind, and I peel it from my shoulders, letting it trail behind me like a flag and then letting it go. I push the sleeves of my shirt up to my elbows as I run, slowing to a jog when my body can no longer stand the sprint. It feels like the entire city is rushing past me in a blur, the buildings blending together. I hear the slap of my shoes like the sound is separate from me.

Finally I have to stop, my muscles burning. I'm in the factionless wasteland that lies between the Abnegation sector and Erudite headquarters, Candor headquarters, and our common places. At every faction meeting, our leaders, usually speaking through my father, urge us not to be afraid of the factionless, to treat them like human beings instead of broken, lost creatures. But it never occurred to me to be afraid of them.

I move to the sidewalk so I can look through the windows of the buildings. Most of the time all I see is old furniture, every room bare, bits of trash on the floor. When most of the city's residents left—as they must have, since our current population doesn't fill every building—they must not have left in a hurry, because the spaces they occupied are so clean. Nothing of interest remains.

When I pass one of the buildings on the corner, though, I see something inside. The room just beyond the window is as bare as any of the others I've walked by, but past the doorway inside I can see a single ember, a lit coal.

I frown and pause in front of the window to see if it will open. At first it won't budge, and then I wiggle it back and forth, and it springs upward. I push my torso through first, and then my legs, toppling to the ground inside in a heap of limbs. My elbows sting as they scrape the floor.

The building smells like cooked food and smoke and sweat. I inch toward the ember, listening for voices that will warn me of a factionless presence here, but there's only silence.

In the next room, the windows are blacked out by paint and dirt, but a little daylight makes it through them, so I can see that there are curled pallets scattered on the floor all over the room, and old cans with bits of dried food stuck inside them. In the center of the room is a small charcoal grill. Most of the coals are white, their fuel spent, but one is still lit, suggesting that whoever was here was here recently. And judging by the smell and the abundance of old cans and blankets, there were quite a few of them.

I was always taught that the factionless lived without community, isolated from one another. Now, looking at this place, I wonder why I ever believed it. What would be stopping them from forming groups, just like we have? It's in our nature.

"What are you doing here?" a voice demands, and it travels through me like an electric shock. I wheel around and see a smudged, sallow-faced man in the next room, wiping his hands on a ragged towel.

"I was just . . ." I look at the grill. "I saw fire. That's all."

"Oh." The man tucks the corner of the towel into his back pocket. He wears black Candor pants, patched with blue Erudite fabric, and a gray Abnegation shirt, the same as the one I'm wearing. He's lean as a rail, but he looks strong. Strong enough to hurt me, but I don't think he will.

"Thanks, I guess," he says. "Nothing's on fire here, though."

"I can see that," I say. "What is this place?"

"It's my house," he says with a cold smile. He's missing one of his teeth. "I didn't know I would be having guests, so I didn't bother to tidy up."

I look from him to the scattered cans. "You must toss and turn a lot, to require so many blankets."

"Never met a Stiff who pried so much into other people's business," he says. He moves closer to me and frowns. "You look a little familiar."

I know I can't have met him before, not where I live, surrounded by identical houses in the most monotonous neighborhood in the city, surrounded by people in identical gray clothing with identical short hair. Then it occurs to me: hidden as my father tries to keep me, he's still the leader of the council, one of the most prominent people in our city, and I still resemble him.

"I'm sorry to have bothered you," I say in my best Abnegation voice. "I'll be going now."

"I do know you," the man says. "You're Evelyn Eaton's son, aren't you?"

I stiffen at her name. It's been years since I heard it, because my father won't speak it, won't even acknowledge it if he hears it. To be connected to her again, even just in facial resemblance, feels strange, like putting on an old piece of clothing that doesn't quite fit anymore.

"How did you know her?" He must have known her

well, to see her in my face, which is paler than hers, the eyes blue instead of dark brown. Most people didn't look closely enough to see all the things we had in common: our long fingers, our hooked noses, our straight, frowned eyebrows.

He hesitates a little. "She volunteered with the Abnegation sometimes. Handing out food and blankets and clothes. Had a memorable face. Plus, she was married to a council leader. Didn't everyone know her?"

Sometimes I know people are lying just because of the way the words feel when they press into me, uncomfortable and wrong, the way an Erudite feels when she reads a grammatically incorrect sentence. However he knew my mother, it's not because she handed him a can of soup once. But I'm so thirsty to hear more about her that I don't press the issue.

"She died, did you know?" I say. "Years ago."

"No, I didn't know." His mouth slants a little at one corner. "I'm sorry to hear that."

I feel strange, standing in this dank place that smells like live bodies and smoke, among these empty cans that suggest poverty and the failure to fit in. But there is something appealing about it here too, a freedom, a refusal to belong to these arbitrary categories we've made for ourselves.

"Your Choosing must be coming up tomorrow, for you to look so worried," the man says. "What faction did you get?"

"I'm not supposed to tell anyone," I say automatically.

"I'm not anyone," he says. "I'm nobody. That's what being factionless is."

I still don't say anything. The prohibition against sharing my aptitude test result, or any of my other secrets, is set firmly in the mold that makes me and remakes me daily. It's impossible to change now.

"Ah, a rule follower," he says, like he's disappointed. "Your mother said to me once that she felt like inertia had carried her to Abnegation. It was the path of least resistance." He shrugs. "Trust me when I tell you, Eaton boy, that resisting is worth doing."

I feel a rush of anger. He shouldn't be telling me about my mother like she belongs to him and not to me, shouldn't be making me question everything I remember about her just because she may or may not have served him food once. He shouldn't be telling me anything at all—he's nobody, factionless, separate, nothing.

"Yeah?" I say. "Look where resisting got you. Living out of cans in broken-down buildings. Doesn't sound so great to me." I start toward the doorway the man emerged from. I know I'll find an alley door somewhere back there;

I don't care where as long as I can get out of here quickly.

I pick a path across the floor, careful not to step on any of the blankets. When I reach the hallway, the man says, "I'd rather eat out of a can than be strangled by a faction."

I don't look back.

+ + +

When I get home, I sit on the front step and take deep breaths of the cool spring air for a few minutes.

My mother was the one who taught me to steal moments like these, moments of freedom, though she didn't know it. I watched her take them, slipping out the door after dark when my father was asleep, creeping back home when sunlight was just appearing behind the buildings. She took them even when she was with us, standing over the sink with her eyes closed, so distant from the present that she didn't even hear me when I spoke to her.

But I learned something else from watching her too, which is that the free moments always have to end.

I get up, brushing flecks of cement from my gray slacks, and push the door open. My father sits in the easy chair in the living room, surrounded by paperwork. I pull up straight, tall, so that he can't scold me for slouching. I move toward the stairs. Maybe he will let me go to my room unnoticed.

"Tell me about your aptitude test," he says, and he points at the sofa for me to sit.

I cross the room, stepping carefully over a stack of papers on the carpet, and sit where he points, right on the edge of the cushion so I can stand up quickly.

"Well?" He removes his glasses and looks at me expectantly. I hear tension in his voice, the kind that only develops after a difficult day at work. I should be careful. "What was your result?"

I don't even think about refusing to tell him. "Abnegation."

"And nothing else?"

I frown. "No, of course not."

"Don't give me that look," he says, and my frown disappears. "Nothing strange happened with your test?"

During my test, I knew where I was—I knew that while I felt like I was standing in the cafeteria of my secondary school, I was actually lying prostrate on a chair in the aptitude test room, my body connected to a machine by a series of wires. That was strange. But I don't want to talk to him about it now, not when I can see the stress brewing inside him like a storm.

"No," I say.

"Don't lie to me," he says, and he seizes my arm, his fingers tight like a vise. I don't look at him.

"I'm not," I say. "I got Abnegation, just as expected. The woman barely looked at me on my way out of the room. I promise."

He releases me. My skin pulses from where he gripped it.

"Good," he says. "I'm sure you have some thinking to do. You should go to your room."

"Yes, sir."

I get up and cross the room again, relieved.

"Oh," he says. "Some of my fellow council members are coming over tonight, so you should eat dinner early."

"Yes, sir."

+ + +

Before the sun goes down, I snatch food from the cupboards and the refrigerator: two dinner rolls and raw carrots with the greens still attached, a hunk of cheese and an apple, leftover chicken without any seasoning on it. The food all tastes the same, like dust and paste. I keep my eyes fixed on the door so I don't collide with my father's coworkers. He wouldn't like it if I was still down here when they came.

I am finishing off a glass of water when the first council member appears on the doorstep, and I hurry through the living room before my father reaches the door. He waits with his hand on the knob, his eyebrows raised at me as I slip around the banister. He points up the stairs and I climb them, fast, as he opens the door.

"Hello, Marcus." I recognize the voice as Andrew Prior's. He's one of my father's closest friends at work, which means nothing, because no one *really* knows my father. Not even me.

From the top of the stairs I look down at Andrew. He's wiping his shoes on the mat. I see him and his family sometimes, a perfect Abnegation unit, Natalie and Andrew, and the son and daughter—not twins, but both two years younger than I am in school—all walking sedately down the sidewalk and bobbing their heads at passersby. Natalie organizes all the factionless volunteer efforts among the Abnegation—my mother must have known her, though she rarely attended Abnegation social events, preferring to keep her secrets like I keep mine, hidden away in this house.

Andrew meets my eyes, and I rush down the hallway to my bedroom, closing the door behind me.

To all appearances, my room is as sparse and clean as every other Abnegation room. My gray sheets and blankets are tucked tightly around the thin mattress, and my schoolbooks are stacked in a perfect tower on my plywood desk. A small dresser that contains several identical sets of clothing stands next to the small window, which lets in only the barest sliver of sunlight in the evenings. Through it I can see the house next door, which is just the same as the one I'm in, except five feet to the east.

I know how inertia carried my mother to Abnegation, if indeed that man was speaking the truth about what she'd told him. I can see it happening to me, too, tomorrow when I stand among the bowls of faction elements with a knife in my hand. There are four factions I don't know or trust, with practices I don't understand, and only one that is familiar, predictable, comprehensible. If choosing Abnegation won't lead me to a life of ecstatic happiness, at least it will lead me to a comfortable place.

I sit on the edge of the bed. *No, it won't,* I think, and then I swallow the thought down, because I know where it comes from: the childish part of me that is afraid of the man holding court in the living room. The man whose knuckles I know better than his embrace.

I make sure the door is closed and wedge the desk chair under the knob just in case. Then I crouch next to the bed and reach under it to the trunk I keep there.

My mother gave it to me when I was young, and told my father it was for spare blankets, that she had found it in an alley somewhere. But when she put it in my room, she didn't fill it with spare blankets. She closed my door and touched her fingers to her lips and set it on my bed to open it.

Inside the unlocked trunk was a blue sculpture. It looked like falling water, but it was really glass, perfectly clear, polished, flawless.

"What does it do?" I asked her at the time.

"It doesn't do anything obvious," she said, and she smiled, but the smile was tight, like she was afraid of something. "But it might be able to do something in here." She tapped her chest, right over the sternum. "Beautiful things sometimes do."

Since then I have filled the trunk with objects that others would call useless: old spectacles without glass in them, fragments of discarded motherboards, spark plugs, stripped wires, the broken neck of a green bottle, a rusted knife blade. I don't know if my mother would have called them beautiful, or even if I would, but each of them struck me the same way that sculpture did, as secret things, and valuable ones, if only because they were so overlooked.

Instead of thinking about my aptitude test result, I pick up each object and turn it in my hands so I've memorized every part of every one.

+++

I wake with a start to Marcus's footsteps in the hallway just outside the bedroom. I'm lying on the bed with the objects strewn on the mattress around me. His footsteps are slowing down as he comes closer to the door, and I pick up the spark plugs and motherboard pieces and wires and throw them back into the trunk and lock it, stowing the key in my pocket. I realize at the last second, as the doorknob starts to move, that the sculpture is still out, so I shove it under the pillow and slide the trunk under the bed.

Then I dive toward the chair and pull it from under the knob so my father can enter.

When he does, he eyes the chair in my hands with suspicion.

"What was that doing over here?" he says. "Are you trying to keep me out?"

"No, sir."

"That's the second time you've lied to me today," Marcus says. "I didn't raise my son to be a liar."

"I—" I can't think of a single thing to say, so I just close my mouth and carry the chair back to my desk where it belongs, right behind the perfect stack of schoolbooks.

"What were you doing in here that you didn't want me to see?"

I clutch the back of the chair, hard, and stare at my books.

"Nothing," I say quietly.

"That's three lies," he says, and his voice is low but hard as flint. He starts toward me, and I back up instinctively. But instead of reaching for me, he bends down and pulls the trunk from beneath the bed, then tries the lid. It doesn't budge.

Fear slides into my gut like a blade. I pinch the hem of my shirt, but I can't feel my fingertips.

"Your mother claimed this was for blankets," he says. "Said you got cold at night. But what I've always wondered is, if it still has blankets in it, why do you keep it locked?"

He holds out his hand, palm up, and raises his eyebrows at me. I know what he wants—the key. And I have to give it to him, because he can see when I'm lying; he can see everything about me. I reach into my pocket, then drop the key in his hand. Now I can't feel my palms, and the breathing is starting, the shallow breathing that always comes when I know he's about to explode.

I close my eyes as he opens the trunk.

"What is this?" His hand moves through the treasured objects carelessly, scattering them to the left and right. He takes them out one by one and thrusts them toward me. "What do you need with *this*, or *this* . . . !"

I flinch, over and over again, and don't have an answer. I don't need them. I don't need any of them.

"This is *rank* with self-indulgence!" he shouts, and he shoves the trunk off the edge of the bed so its contents scatter all over the floor. "It poisons this house with selfishness!"

I can't feel my face, either.

His hands collide with my chest. I stumble back and hit the dresser. Then he draws his hand back by his face to hit me, and I say, my throat tight with fear, "The Choosing Ceremony, Dad!"

He pauses with his hand raised, and I *cower*, shrinking back against the dresser, my eyes too blurry to see out of. He usually tries not to bruise my face, especially for days like tomorrow, when so many people will be staring at me, watching me choose.

He lowers his hand, and for a second I think the violence is over, the anger stalled. But then he says, "Fine. Stay here."

I sag against the dresser. I know better than to think he'll leave and mull things over and come back apologizing. He never does that.

He will return with a belt, and the stripes he carves into my back will be easily hidden by a shirt and an obedient Abnegation expression.

I turn around, a shudder claiming my body. I clutch the edge of the dresser and wait.

+ + +

That night I sleep on my stomach, pain biting each thought, with my broken possessions on the floor around me. After he hit me until I had to stuff my fist into my mouth to muffle a scream, he stomped on each object until it was broken or dented beyond recognition, then threw the trunk into the wall so the lid broke from the hinges.

The thought surfaces: *If you choose Abnegation, you will never get away from him.*

I push my face into my pillow.

But I'm not strong enough to resist this Abnegation-inertia, this fear that drives me down the path my father has set for me.

+ + +

The next morning I take a cold shower, not to conserve resources as the Abnegation instruct, but because it numbs my back. I dress slowly in my loose, plain Abnegation clothes, and stand in front of the hallway mirror to cut my hair.

"Let me," my father says from the end of the hallway. "It's your Choosing Day, after all."

I set the clippers down on the ledge created by the sliding panel and try to straighten up. He stands behind me, and I avert my eyes as the clippers start to buzz. There's only one guard for the blade, only one length of hair acceptable for an Abnegation male. I wince as his fingers stabilize my head, and hope he doesn't see it, doesn't see how even his slightest touch terrifies me.

"You know what to expect," he says. He covers the top of my ear with one hand as he drags the clippers over the side of my head. Today he's trying to protect my ear from getting nicked by clippers, and yesterday he took a belt to me. The thought feels like poison working through me. It's almost funny. I almost want to laugh.

"You'll stand in your place; when your name is called, you'll go forward to get your knife. Then you'll cut yourself and drop the blood into the right bowl." Our eyes meet in the mirror, and he presses his mouth into a near-smile. He touches my shoulder, and I realize that we are about the same height now, about the same size, though I still feel so much smaller.

Then he adds gently, "The knife will only hurt for a moment. Then your choice will be made, and it will all be over."

I wonder if he even remembers what happened yesterday, or if he's already shoved it into a separate compartment in his mind, keeping his monster half separate from his father half. But I don't have those compartments, and I can see all his identities layered over one another, monster and father and man and council leader and widower.

And suddenly my heart is pounding so hard, my face is so hot, I can barely stand it.

"Don't worry about me handling the pain," I say. "I've had a lot of practice."

For a second his eyes are like daggers in the mirror, and my strong anger is gone, replaced by familiar fear. But all he does is switch off the clippers and set them on the ledge and walk down the stairs, leaving me to sweep up the trimmed hair, to brush it from my shoulders and neck, to put the clippers away in their drawer in the bathroom.

Then I go back into my room and stare at the broken objects on the floor. Carefully, I gather them into a pile and put them in the wastebasket next to my desk, piece by piece.

Wincing, I come to my feet. My legs are shaking.

In that moment, staring at the bare life I've made for myself here, at the destroyed remnants of what little I had, I think, *I have to get out.*

It's a strong thought. I feel its strength ringing inside me like the toll of a bell, so I think it again. *I have to get out.*

I walk toward the bed and slide my hand under the pillow, where my mother's sculpture is still safe, still blue and gleaming with morning light. I put it on my desk, next to the stack of books, and leave my bedroom, closing the door behind me.

Downstairs, I'm too nervous to eat, but I stuff a piece of toast into my mouth anyway so my father won't ask me any questions. I shouldn't worry. Now he's pretending I don't exist, pretending I'm not flinching every time I have to bend down to pick something up.

I have to get out. It's a chant now, a mantra, the only thing I have left to hold on to.

He finishes reading the news the Erudite release every morning, and I finish washing my own dishes, and we walk out of the house together without speaking. We walk down the sidewalk, and he greets our neighbors with a smile, and everything is always in perfect order for Marcus Eaton, except for his son. Except for me; I am not in order, I am in constant disarray.

But today, I'm glad for that.

We get on the bus and stand in the aisle to let others sit down around us, the perfect picture of Abnegation deference. I watch the others get on, Candor boys and girls with loud mouths, Erudite with studious stares. I watch the other Abnegation rise from their seats to give them away. Everyone is going to the same place today—the Hub, a black pillar in the distance, its two prongs stabbing the sky.

When we get there, my father puts a hand on my shoulder as we walk to the entrance, sending shocks of pain through my body.

I have to get out.

It's a desperate thought, and the pain only spurs it on with each footstep as I walk the stairs to the Choosing Ceremony floor. I struggle for air, but it's not because of my aching legs; it's because of my weak heart, growing stronger with each passing second. Beside me, Marcus wipes beads of sweat from his forehead, and all the other Abnegation close their lips to keep from breathing too loudly, lest they appear to be complaining.

I lift my eyes to the stairs ahead of me, and I am on fire with this thought, this need, this chance to escape.

We reach the right floor, and everyone pauses to catch their breath before entering. The room is dim, the windows blocked off, the seats arranged around the circle of bowls that hold glass and water and stones and coal and earth. I find my place in line, between an Abnegation girl and an Amity boy. Marcus stands in front of me.

"You know what to do," he says, and it's more like he's

telling himself than me. "You know what the right choice is. I know you do."

I just stare somewhere south of his eyes.

"I'll see you soon," he says.

He moves toward the Abnegation section and sits in the front row, with some of the other council leaders. Gradually people fill the room, those who are about to choose standing in a square at the edge, those watching sitting in the chairs in the middle. The doors close, and there's a moment of quiet as the council representative from Dauntless moves to the podium. Max is his name. He wraps his fingers around the edge of the podium, and I can see, even from here, that his knuckles are bruised.

Do they learn to fight in Dauntless? They must.

"Welcome to the Choosing Ceremony," Max says, his deep voice filling the room easily. He doesn't need the microphone; his voice is loud enough and strong enough to penetrate my skull and wrap around my brain. "Today you will choose your factions. Until this point you have followed your parents' paths, your parents' rules. Today you will find your own path, make your own rules."

I can almost see my father pressing his lips together with disdain at such a typical Dauntless speech. I know his habits so well, I almost do it myself, though I don't share the feeling. I have no particular opinions about Dauntless.

"A long time ago our ancestors realized that each of us, each individual, was responsible for the evil that exists in the world. But they didn't agree on exactly what that evil was," Max says. "Some said that it was dishonesty. . . ."

I think of the lies I have told, year after year, about this bruise or that cut, the lies of omission I told when I kept Marcus's secrets.

"Some said that it was ignorance, some aggression. . . ."

I think of the peace of the Amity orchards, the freedom I would find there from violence and cruelty.

"Some said selfishness was the cause."

This is for your own good is what Marcus said before the first blow fell. As if hitting me was an act of self-sacrifice. As if it hurt him to do it. Well, I didn't see *him* limping around the kitchen this morning.

"And the last group said that it was cowardice that was to blame."

A few hoots rise up from the Dauntless section, and the rest of the Dauntless laugh. I think of the fear swallowing me last night until I couldn't feel, until I couldn't breathe. I think of the years that have ground me into dust beneath my father's heel.

"That is how we came by our factions: Candor, Erudite,

Amity, Abnegation, and Dauntless." Max smiles. "In them we find administrators and teachers and counselors and leaders and protectors. In them we find our sense of belonging, our sense of community, our very lives." He clears his throat. "Enough of that. Let's get to it. Come forward and get your knife, then make your choice. First up, Zellner, Gregory."

It seems fitting that pain should follow me from my old life into my new one, with the knife digging into my palm. Still, even this morning I didn't know which faction I would choose as a haven. Gregory Zellner holds his bleeding hand over the bowl of dirt, to choose Amity.

Amity seems like the obvious choice for a haven, with its peaceful life, its sweet-smelling orchards, its smiling community. In Amity I would find the kind of acceptance I've craved my entire life, and maybe, over time, it would teach me to feel steady in myself, comfortable with who I am.

But as I look at the people sitting in that section, in their reds and yellows, I see only whole, healed people, capable of cheering one another, capable of supporting one another. They are too perfect, too kind, for someone like me to be driven into their arms by rage and fear.

The ceremony is moving too fast. "Rogers, Helena."

She chooses Candor.

I know what happens in Candor's initiation. I heard whispers about it in school one day. There, I would have to expose every secret, dig it out with my fingernails. I would have to flay myself alive to join Candor. No, I can't do that.

"Lovelace, Frederick."

Frederick Lovelace, dressed all in blue, cuts his palm and lets his blood drip into the Erudite water, turning it a deeper shade of pink. I learn easily enough for Erudite, but I know myself well enough to understand that I am too volatile, too emotional, for a place like that. It would strangle me, and what I want is to be free, not to be shuffled into yet another prison.

It takes no time at all for the name of the Abnegation girl beside me to be called. "Erasmus, Anne."

Anne—another one who never found more than a few words to speak to me—stumbles forward and walks the aisle to Max's podium. She accepts her knife with shaking hands and cuts her palm, and holds her hand over the Abnegation bowl. It's easy for her. She doesn't have anything to run from, just a welcoming, kind community to rejoin. And besides, no one from Abnegation has transferred in years. It's the most loyal faction, in terms of Choosing Ceremony statistics.

"Eaton, Tobias."

I don't feel nervous as I walk down the aisle to the bowls, though I still haven't chosen my place. Max passes me the knife, and I wrap my fingers around the handle. It's smooth and cool, the blade clean. A new knife for each person, and a new choice.

As I walk to the center of the room, to the center of the bowls, I pass Tori, the woman who administered my aptitude test. *You're the one who has to live with your choice,* she said. Her hair is pulled back, and I can see a tattoo creeping over her collarbone, toward her throat. Her eyes touch mine with peculiar force, and I stare back, unflinching, as I take my place among the bowls.

What choice can I live with? Not Erudite, or Candor. Not Abnegation, the place I am trying to get away from. Not even Amity, where I am too broken to belong.

The truth is, I want my choice to drive a knife right through my father's heart, to pierce him with as much pain and embarrassment and disappointment as possible.

There is only one choice that can do that.

I look at him, and he nods, and I cut deep into my own palm, so deep the pain brings tears to my eyes. I blink them away and curl my hand into a fist to let the blood collect there. His eyes are like my eyes, such a dark blue that in light like this they always look black, just pits in his skull. My back throbs and pinches, my collared shirt scratching at the raw skin there, the skin he wore into with that belt.

I open my palm over the coals. I feel like they're burning in my stomach, filling me to the brim with fire and smoke.

I am free.

+ + +

I don't hear the cheers of the Dauntless; all I hear is ringing.

My new faction is like a many-armed creature, stretching toward me. I move toward it, and I don't dare to look back to see my father's face. Hands slap my arms, commending me on my choice, and I move to the rear of the group, blood wrapping around my fingers.

I stand with the other initiates, next to a black-haired Erudite boy who appraises and dismisses me with one glance. I must not look like much, in my Abnegation grays, tall and scrawny after last year's growth spurt. The cut in my hand is gushing, the blood spilling onto the floor and running down my wrist. I dug too deep with the knife.

As the last of my peers choose, I pinch the hem of my loose Abnegation shirt between my fingers and rip. I tear a strip of fabric from the front and wrap it around my hand to stop the bleeding. I won't need these clothes anymore.

The Dauntless sitting in front of us come to their feet as soon as the last person chooses, and they rush toward the doors, carrying me with them. I turn back right before the doors, unable to stop myself, and I see my father sitting in the front row still, a few other Abnegation huddled around him. He looks stunned.

I smirk a little. I did it, *I* put that expression on his face. I am not the perfect Abnegation child, doomed to be swallowed whole by the system and dissolved into obscurity. Instead, I am the first Abnegation-Dauntless transfer in more than a decade.

I turn and run to catch up with the others, not wanting to be left behind. Before I exit the room, I unbutton my ripped long-sleeved shirt and let it fall on the ground. The gray T-shirt I am wearing beneath it is still oversized, but it's darker, blends in better with the black Dauntless clothes.

They storm down the stairs, flinging doors open, laughing, shouting. I feel burning in my back and shoulders and lungs and legs, and suddenly I am unsure of this choice I've made, of these people I've claimed. They are so loud and so wild. Can I possibly make a place for myself among them? I don't know.

I guess I don't have a choice.

I push my way through the group, searching for my

fellow initiates, but they seem to have disappeared. I move to the side of the group, hoping to get a glimpse of where we're headed, and I see the train tracks suspended over the street in front of us, in a cage of latticed wood and metal. The Dauntless climb the stairs and spill out onto the train platform. At the foot of the stairs, the crowd is so dense that I can't find a way to get in, but I know if I don't climb the stairs soon, I might miss the train, so I decide to push my way in. I have to clench my teeth to keep myself from apologizing as I elbow people aside, and the momentum of the crowd presses me up the steps.

"You're not a bad runner," Tori says as she sidles up to me on the platform. "At least for an Abnegation kid."

"Thanks," I say.

"You know what's going to happen next, right?" She turns and points at a light in the distance, fixed to the front of an oncoming train. "It's not going to stop. It's just going to slow down a little. And if you don't make it on, that's it for you. Factionless. It's that easy to get kicked out."

I nod. I'm not surprised that the trial of initiation has already begun, that it began the second we left the Choosing Ceremony. And I'm not surprised that the Dauntless expect me to prove myself either. I watch the train come closer—I can hear it now, whistling on the tracks.

She grins at me. "You're going to do just fine here, aren't you?"

"What makes you say that?"

She shrugs. "You strike me as someone who's ready to fight, that's all."

The train thunders toward us, and the Dauntless start piling on. Tori runs toward the edge, and I follow her, copying her stance and her movements as she prepares to jump. She grabs a handle at the edge of the door and swings herself inside, so I do the same thing, fumbling at first for my grip and then yanking myself in.

But I'm unprepared for the turning of the train, and I stumble, smacking my face against the metal wall. I grab my aching nose.

"Smooth," one of the Dauntless inside says. He's younger than Tori, with dark skin and an easy smile.

"Finesse is for Erudite show-offs," Tori says. "He made it on the train, Amar, that's what counts."

"He's supposed to be in the other car, though. With the other initiates," Amar says. He eyes me, but not the way the Erudite transfer did a few minutes ago. He seems more curious than anything else, like I'm an oddity he needs to examine carefully in order to understand it. "If he's friends with you, I guess it's okay. What's your name, Stiff?"

The name is in my mouth the second he asks me the question, and I am about to answer like I always do, that I am Tobias Eaton. It should be natural, but in that moment I can't bear to say my name out loud, not here, among the people I hoped would be my new friends, my new family. I can't—I *won't*—be Marcus Eaton's son anymore.

"You can call me 'Stiff' for all I care," I say, trying out the cutting Dauntless banter I've only listened to across hallways and classrooms until now. Wind rushes into the train car as it picks up speed, and it's *loud*, roaring in my ears.

Tori gives me a strange look, and for a moment I am afraid that she's going to tell Amar my name, which I'm sure she remembers from my aptitude test. But she just nods a little, and relieved, I turn toward the open doorway, my hand still on the handle.

It never occurred to me before that I could refuse to give my name, or that I could give a false one, construct a new identity for myself. I'm free here, free to snap at people and free to refuse them and free even to lie.

I see the street between the wooden beams that support the train tracks, just a story beneath us. But up ahead, the old tracks give way to new ones, and the platforms go higher, wrapping around the roofs of buildings. The climb happens gradually, so I wouldn't have noticed it was happening if I hadn't been staring at the ground as we traveled farther and farther away from it, farther and farther into the sky.

Fear makes my legs go weak, so I back away from the doorway and sink into a crouch by one wall as I wait to get to wherever we're going.

+ + +

I am still in that position—crouched by the wall, my head in my hands—when Amar nudges me with his foot.

"Get up, Stiff," he says, not unkindly. "It's almost time to jump."

"Jump?" I say.

"Yeah." He smirks. "This train stops for no one."

I press myself up. The fabric I wrapped around my hand is soaked through with red. Tori stands right behind me and pushes me toward the doorway.

"Let the initiate off first!" she shouts.

"What are you doing?" I demand, scowling at her.

"I'm doing you a favor!" she answers, and she shoves me toward the opening again. The other Dauntless step back for me, each one of them grinning like I'm a meal. I shuffle toward the edge, grabbing the handle so hard the tips of my fingers start to go numb. I see where I'm supposed to jump—up ahead, the tracks hug the roof of a building and then turn. The gap looks small from here, but as the train gets closer, it seems larger and larger, and my imminent death seems more and more likely.

My entire body shakes as the Dauntless in the cars ahead of us make the jump. None of them miss the roof, but that doesn't mean I won't be the first. I pry my fingers from the handle and stare at the rooftop and push off as hard as I can.

The impact shudders through me, and I fall forward onto my hands and knees, the gravel on the roof digging into my wounded palm. I stare at my fingers. I feel like time just lurched forward, the actual jump disappearing from sight and memory.

"Damn," someone behind me says. "I was hoping we would get to scrape some Stiff pancake off the pavement later."

I glare at the ground and sit back on my heels. The roof is tilting and bobbing beneath me—I didn't know a person could be dizzy with fear.

Still, I know I just passed two initiation tests: I got on a moving train, and I made it to the roof. Now the question is, how do the Dauntless get *off* the roof?

A moment later Amar steps up on the ledge, and I have my answer:

They're going to make us jump.

I close my eyes and pretend that I'm not here, kneeling on this gravel with these insane ink-marked people surrounding me. I came here to escape, but this is not an escape, it's just a different kind of torture and it's too late to get out of it. My only hope, then, is to survive it.

"Welcome to Dauntless!" Amar shouts. "Where you either face your fears and try not to die in the process, or you leave a coward. We've got a record low of faction transfers this year, unsurprisingly."

The Dauntless around Amar punch the air and whoop, bearing the fact that no one wants to join them as a banner of pride.

"The only way to get into the Dauntless compound from this rooftop is to jump off this ledge," Amar says, opening his arms wide to indicate the empty space around him. He tilts back on his heels and waves his arms around, like he's about to fall, then catches himself and grins. I pull a deep breath in through my nose and hold it.

"As usual, I offer the opportunity to go first to our initiates, Dauntless-born or not." He hops down from the ledge and gestures to it, eyebrows raised.

The cluster of young Dauntless near the roof exchange looks. Standing off to the side are the Erudite boy from before, an Amity girl, two Candor boys, and a Candor girl. There are only six of us.

One of the Dauntless steps up, a dark-skinned boy who beckons cheers from his friends with his hands.

"Go, Zeke!" one of the girls shouts.

Zeke hops onto the ledge but misjudges the jump and tips forward right away, losing his balance. He yells something unintelligible and disappears. The Candor girl nearby gasps, covering her mouth with one hand, but Zeke's Dauntless friends burst into laughter. I don't think that was the dramatic, heroic moment he had in mind.

Amar, grinning, gestures to the ledge again. The Dauntless-borns line up behind it, and so do the Erudite boy and the Amity girl. I know I have to join them, I have to jump, it doesn't matter how I feel about it. I move toward the line, stiff like my joints are rusted bolts. Amar looks at his watch and cues each jumper at thirty-second intervals.

The line is shrinking, dissolving.

Suddenly it's gone, and I am all that is left. I step onto the ledge and wait for Amar's cue. The sun is setting behind the buildings in the distance, their jagged line unfamiliar from this angle. The light glows gold near the horizon, and wind rushes up the side of the building, lifting my clothes away from my body.

"Go ahead," Amar says.

I close my eyes, and I'm frozen; I can't even push myself

off the roof. All I can do is tilt and fall. My stomach drops and my limbs fumble in the air for something, anything to hold on to, but there is nothing, only the drop, the air, the frantic search for the ground.

Then I hit a net.

It curls around me, wrapping me in strong threads. Hands beckon to me from the edge. I hook my fingers in the net and pull myself toward them. I land on my feet on a wooden platform, and a man with dark brown skin and bruised knuckles grins at me. Max.

"The Stiff!" He claps me on the back, making me flinch. "Nice to see you made it this far. Go join your fellow initiates. Amar will be down in a second, I'm sure."

Behind him is a dark tunnel with rock walls. The Dauntless compound is underground—I assumed it would be dangling from a high building from a series of flimsy ropes, a manifestation of my worst nightmares.

I try to walk down the steps and over to the other transfers. My legs seem to be working again. The Amity girl smiles at me. "That was surprisingly fun," she says. "I'm Mia. You okay?"

"It looks like he's trying not to throw up," one of the Candor boys says.

"Just let it happen, man," the other Candor boy adds. "We'd love to see a show."

My response comes out of nowhere. "Shut up," I snap.

To my surprise, they do. I guess they haven't been told to shut up by many of the Abnegation.

A few seconds later, I see Amar rolling over the edge of the net. He descends the steps, looking wild and rumpled and ready for the next insane stunt. He beckons all the initiates closer to him, and we gather at the opening of the yawning tunnel in a semicircle.

Amar brings his hands together in front of him.

"My name is Amar," he says. "I'm your initiation instructor. I grew up here, and three years ago, I passed initiation with flying colors, which means I get to be in charge of the newcomers for as long as I want. Lucky you.

"Dauntless-borns and transfers do most physical training separately, so that the Dauntless-borns don't break the transfers in half right away—" At this, the Dauntless-borns on the other side of the semicircle grin. "But we're trying something different this year. The Dauntless leaders and I want to see if knowing your fears before you begin training will better prepare you for the rest of initiation. So before we even let you into the dining hall to have dinner, we're going to do some self-discovery. Follow me."

"What if I don't want to discover myself?" Zeke asks.

All Amar has to do is look at him for him to sink back

into the group of Dauntless-borns again. Amar is like no one I've ever met—affable one minute and stern the next, and sometimes both at once.

He leads the way down the tunnel, then stops at a door built into the wall and shoves it open with his shoulder. We follow him into a dank room with a giant window in the back wall. Above us the fluorescent lights flicker and twitch, and Amar busies himself at a machine that looks a lot like the one used to administer my aptitude test. I hear a dripping sound—water from the ceiling is leaking into a puddle in the corner.

Another large, empty room stretches out beyond the window. There are cameras in each corner—are there cameras all over the Dauntless compound?

"This is the fear landscape room," Amar announces without looking up. "A fear landscape is a simulation in which you confront your worst fears."

Arranged on the table next to the machine is a line of syringes. They look sinister to me in the flickering light, like they might as well be instruments of torture, knives and blades and hot pokers.

"How is that possible?" the Erudite boy says. "You don't know our worst fears."

"Eric, right?" Amar says. "You're correct, I don't know your worst fears, but the serum I am going to inject you with will stimulate the parts of your brain that process fear, and you will come up with the simulation obstacles yourself, so to speak. In this simulation, unlike in the aptitude test simulation, you will be aware that what you are seeing is not real. Meanwhile, I will be in this room, controlling the simulation, and I get to tell the program embedded in the simulation serum to move on to the next obstacle once your heart rate reaches a particular level—once you calm down, in other words, or face your fear in a significant way. When you run out of fears, the program will terminate and you will 'wake up' in that room again with a greater awareness of your own fears."

He picks up one of the syringes and beckons to Eric.

"Allow me to satisfy your Erudite curiosity," he says. "You get to go first."

"But—"

"But," Amar says smoothly, "I am your initiation instructor, and it's in your best interest to do as I say."

Eric stands still for a moment, then removes his blue jacket, folds it in half, and drapes it over the back of a chair. His movements are slow and deliberate—designed, I suspect, to irritate Amar as much as possible. Eric approaches Amar, who sticks the needle almost savagely into the side of Eric's neck. Then he steers Eric toward the next room.

Once Eric is standing in the middle of the room behind the glass, Amar attaches himself to the simulation machine with electrodes and presses something on the computer screen behind it to start the program.

Eric is still, his hands by his sides. He stares at us through the window, and a moment later, though he hasn't moved, it looks like he's staring at something else, like the simulation has begun. But he doesn't scream or thrash or cry, like I would expect of someone who is staring down his worst fears. His heart rate, recorded on the monitor in front of Amar, rises and rises, like a bird taking flight.

He's afraid. He's afraid, but he's not even moving.

"What's going on?" Mia asks me. "Is the serum working?"

I nod.

I watch Eric take a deep breath into his gut and release it through his nose. His body shakes, shivers, like the ground is rumbling beneath him, but his breaths are slow and even, his muscles clenching and then relaxing every few seconds, like he keeps tensing up by accident and then correcting his mistake. I watch his heart rate on the monitor in front of Amar, watch it slow down more and more until Amar taps the screen, forcing the program to move on.

This happens over and over again with each new fear. I

count the fears as they pass in silence, ten, eleven, twelve. Then Amar taps the screen one last time, and Eric's body relaxes. He blinks, slowly, then smirks at the window.

I notice that the Dauntless-borns, usually so quick to comment on everything, are silent. That must mean that what I'm feeling is correct—that Eric is someone to watch out for. Maybe even someone to be afraid of.

+ + +

For more than an hour I watch the other initiates face their fears, running and jumping and aiming invisible guns and, in some cases, lying facedown on the floor, sobbing. Sometimes I get a sense of what they see, of the crawling, creeping fears that torment them, but most of the time the villains they're warding off are private ones, known only to them and Amar.

I stay near the back of the room, shrinking down every time he calls on the next person. But then I'm the last one in the room, and Mia is just finishing, pulled out of her fear landscape when she's crouching against the back wall, her head in her hands. She stands, looking worn, and shuffles out of the room without waiting for Amar to dismiss her. He glances at the last syringe on the table, then at me.

"Just you and me, Stiff," he says. "Come on, let's get this over with."

I stand in front of him. I barely feel the needle go in; I've never had a problem with shots, though some of the other initiates got teary-eyed before the injection. I walk into the next room and face the window, which looks like a mirror on this side. In the moment before the simulation takes effect, I can see myself the way the others must have seen me, slouched and buried in fabric, tall and bony and bleeding. I try to straighten up, and I'm surprised by the difference it makes, surprised by the shadow of strength I see in myself right before the room disappears.

Images fill the space in pieces, the skyline of our city, the hole in the pavement seven stories below me, the line of the ledge beneath my feet. Wind rushes up the side of the building, stronger than it was when I was here in real life, whipping my clothes so hard they snap, and pushing against me from all angles. Then the building grows with me on top of it, moving me far away from the ground. The hole seals up, and hard pavement covers it.

I cringe away from the edge, but the wind won't let me move backward. My heart pounds harder and faster as I confront the reality of what I have to do; I have to jump again, this time not trusting that there won't be pain when I slam into the ground.

A Stiff pancake.

I shake out my hands, squeeze my eyes shut, and

scream into my teeth. Then I follow the push of the wind and I drop, fast. I hit the ground.

Searing, white-hot pain rushes through me, just for a second.

I stand up, wiping dust from my cheek, and wait for the next obstacle. I have no idea what it will be. I haven't taken much time to consider my fears, or even what it would mean to be free from fear, to conquer it. It occurs to me that without fear, I might be strong, powerful, unstoppable. The idea seduces me for just a second before something hits my back, hard.

Then something hits my left side, and my right side, and I'm enclosed in a box large enough only for my body. Shock protects me from panic, at first, and then I breathe the close air and stare into the empty darkness, and my insides squeeze tighter and tighter. I can't breathe anymore. I can't breathe.

I bite down on my lip to keep from sobbing—I don't want Amar to see me cry, don't want him to tell the Dauntless that I'm a coward. I have to think, can't think, through the suffocation of this box. The wall against my back here is the same as the one in my memory, from when I was young, shut in the darkness in the upstairs hallway as punishment. I was never sure when it would end, how many hours I would be stuck there with imaginary monsters creeping up on me in the dark, with the sound of my mother's sobs leaking through the walls.

I slam my hands against the wall in front of me, again and again, then claw at it, though the splinters stab the skin under my fingernails. I put up my forearms and hit the box with the full weight of my body, again and again, closing my eyes so I can pretend I'm not in here, I'm not in here. *Let me out let me out let me out let me out.*

"Think it through, Stiff!" a voice shouts, and I go still. I remember that this is a simulation.

Think it through. What do I need to get out of this box? I need a tool, something stronger than I am. I nudge something with my toes and reach down to pick it up. But when I reach down, the top of the box moves with me, and I can't straighten again. I swallow a scream and find the pointy end of a crowbar with my fingers. I wedge it between the boards that form the left corner of the box and push as hard as I can.

All the boards spring apart at once and fall on the ground around me. I breathe the fresh air, relieved.

Then a woman appears in front of me. I don't recognize her face, and her clothes are white, not belonging to any faction. I move toward her, and a table springs up in front of me, with a gun and a bullet on it. I frown at it.

Is this a fear?

"Who are you?" I ask her, and she doesn't answer.

It's clear what I'm supposed to do—load the gun, fire the bullet. Dread builds inside of me, as powerful as any fear. My mouth goes dry, and I fumble for the bullet and the gun. I've never held a gun before, so it takes me a few seconds to figure out how to open the chamber of the pistol. In those seconds I think of the light leaving her eyes, this woman I don't know, don't know enough to care about her.

I am afraid—I am afraid of what I will be asked to do in Dauntless, of what I will want to do.

Afraid of some kind of hidden violence inside of me, wrought by my father and by the years of silence my faction forced on me.

I slide the bullet into the chamber, then hold the gun in both hands, the cut in my palm throbbing. I look at the woman's face. Her lower lip wobbles, and her eyes fill with tears.

"I'm sorry," I say, and I pull the trigger.

I see the dark hole the bullet creates in her body, and she falls to the floor, evaporating into a cloud of dust on contact.

But the dread doesn't go away. I know that something's coming; I can feel it building inside me. Marcus has not appeared yet, and he will, I know it as surely as I know my own name. Our name.

A circle of light envelops me, and at its edge, I see worn gray shoes pacing. Marcus Eaton steps into the edge of the light, but not the Marcus Eaton I know. This one has pits for eyes and a gaping black maw instead of a mouth.

Another Marcus Eaton stands beside him, and slowly, all around the circle, more and more monstrous versions of my father step forward to surround me, their yawning, toothless mouths open wide, their heads tilting at odd angles. I squeeze my hands into fists. It's not real. It's obviously not real.

The first Marcus undoes his belt and then slides it out from around his waist, loop by loop, and as he does, so do the other Marcuses. As they do, the belts turn into ropes made of metal, barbed at the ends. They drag their belts in lines across the floor, their oily black tongues sliding over the edges of their dark mouths. At once they draw back the metal ropes, and I scream at the top of my lungs, wrapping my arms around my head.

"This is for your own good," the Marcuses say in metallic, united voices, like a choir.

I feel pain, tearing, ripping, shredding. I fall to my knees and squeeze my arms against my ears like they can protect me, but nothing can protect me, nothing. I scream again and again but the pain continues, and so does his voice. "I will not have self-indulgent behavior in my house!" "I did not raise my son to be a liar!"

I can't hear, I won't hear.

An image of the sculpture my mother gave me rises into my mind, unbidden. I see it where I placed it on my desk, and the pain starts to recede. I focus all my thoughts on it and the other objects scattered around my room, broken, the top of the trunk loose from its hinges. I remember my mother's hands, with their slim fingers, closing the trunk and locking it and handing me the key.

One by one, the voices disappear, until there are none left.

I let my arms fall to the ground, waiting for the next obstacle. My knuckles brush the stone floor, which is cold and grainy with dirt. I hear footsteps and brace myself for what's coming, but then I hear Amar's voice:

"That's it?" he says. "That's all there is? God, Stiff."

He stops next to me and offers me his hand. I take it and let him pull me to my feet. I don't look at him. I don't want to see his expression. I don't want him to know what he knows, don't want to become the pathetic initiate with the messed-up childhood.

"We should come up with another name for you," he says casually. "Something tougher than 'Stiff.' Like 'Blade' or 'Killer' or something."

At that I do look at him. He's smiling a little. I do see

some pity in that smile, but not as much as I thought I would.

"I wouldn't want to tell people my name either," he says. "Come on, let's get some food."

+ + +

Amar walks me over to the initiates' table once we're in the dining hall. There are a few Dauntless already sitting at the surrounding tables, eyeing the other side of the room, where pierced and tattooed cooks are still setting out the food. The dining hall is a cavern lit from beneath by blue-white lamps, giving everything an eerie glow.

I sit down in one of the empty chairs.

"Jeez, Stiff. You look like you're about to faint," Eric says, and one of the Candor boys grins.

"You all made it out alive," Amar says. "Congratulations. You made it through the first day of initiation, with varying degrees of success." He looks at Eric. "None of you did as well as Four over here, though."

He points at me as he speaks. I frown—four? Is he talking about my fears?

"Hey, Tori," Amar calls over his shoulder. "You ever hear of anyone having only four fears in their fear landscape?"

"Last I heard, the record was seven or eight. Why?" Tori calls back.

"I've got a transfer over here with only four fears."

Tori points at me, and Amar nods.

"That's gotta be a new record," Tori says.

"Well done," Amar says to me. Then he turns and walks toward Tori's table.

All the other initiates stare at me, wide-eyed and quiet. Before the fear landscape, I was just someone they could step on, on their way to Dauntless membership. Now I'm like Eric—someone worth watching out for, maybe even someone worth being afraid of.

Amar gave me more than a new name. He gave me power.

"What's your real name, again? Starts with an *E* . . . ?" Eric asks me, narrowing his eyes. Like he knows something but isn't sure that now is the time to share it.

The others might remember my name too, vaguely, from the Choosing Ceremony, the way I remember theirs—just letters in an alphabet, buried under a nervous haze as I anticipated my own choice. If I strike at their memories now, as hard as I can, become as memorable as my Dauntless self as possible, I can maybe save myself.

I hesitate for a moment, then put my elbows on the table

and raise an eyebrow at him.

"My name is Four," I say. "Call me 'Stiff' again and you and I will have a problem."

He rolls his eyes, but I know I've made myself clear. I have a new name, which means I can be a new person. Someone who doesn't put up with cutting comments from Erudite know-it-alls. Someone who can cut back.

Someone who's finally ready to fight.

Four.

THE INITIATE

THE TRAINING ROOM smells like effort, like sweat and dust and shoes. Every time my fist hits the punching bag it stings my knuckles, which are split open from a week of Dauntless fights.

"So I guess you saw the boards," Amar says, leaning against the door frame. He crosses his arms. "And realized that you're up against Eric tomorrow. Or else you would be in the fear landscape room instead of in here."

"I come in here, too," I say, and I back away from the bag, shaking out my hands. Sometimes I clench my hands so hard I start to lose feeling in my fingertips.

I almost lost my first fight, against the Amity girl, Mia. I didn't know how to beat her without hitting her, and I couldn't hit her—at least, not until she had me in a choke hold and my vision was starting to go black at the edges. My instincts took over, and just one hard elbow to her jaw knocked her down. I still feel guilt curling up inside me when I think about it.

I almost lost the second fight, too, against the bigger Candor boy Sean. I wore him out, crawling to my feet every time he thought I was finished. He didn't know that pushing through pain is one of my oldest habits, learned young, like chewing on my thumbnail, or holding my fork in my left hand instead of my right. Now my face is patchworked with bruises and cuts, but I proved myself.

Tomorrow my opponent is Eric. Beating him will take more than a clever move, or persistence. It will take skill I don't have, strength I haven't earned.

"Yeah, I know." Amar laughs. "See, I spend a lot of time trying to figure out what your deal is, so I've been asking around. Turns out you're in here every morning and in the fear landscape room every night. You never spend any time with the other initiates. You're always exhausted and you sleep like a corpse."

A drop of sweat rolls down the back of my ear. I wipe it away with my taped-up fingers, then drag my arm across my forehead.

"Joining a faction is about more than getting through initiation, you know," Amar says, and he hooks his fingers in the chain that the punching bag dangles from, testing its strength. "For most of the Dauntless, they meet their best friends during initiation, their girlfriends, boyfriends, whatever. Enemies, too. But you seem determined not to have any of those things."

I've seen the other initiates together, getting pierced together and showing up to training with red, studded noses and ears and lips, or building towers out of food scraps at the breakfast table. It never even occurred to me that I could be one of them, or that I should try to be.

I shrug. "I'm used to being alone."

"Well, I feel like you're about to snap, and I don't really want to be there when it happens," he says. "Come on. A bunch of us are going to play a game tonight. A Dauntless game."

I pick at the tape covering one of my knuckles. I shouldn't go out and play games. I should stay here and work, and then sleep, so I'm ready to fight tomorrow.

But that voice, the one that says "should," now sounds to me like my father's voice, requiring me to behave, to isolate myself. And I came here because I was ready to *stop* listening to that voice.

"I'm offering you some Dauntless status for no particular reason other than that I feel bad for you," he says. "Don't be stupid and miss this opportunity."

"Fine," I say. "What's the game?"

Amar just smiles.

+ + +

"The game is Dare." A Dauntless girl, Lauren, is holding on to the handle on the side of the train car, but she keeps swaying so she almost falls out, then giggling and pulling herself back in, like the train isn't suspended two stories above the street, like she wouldn't break her neck if she fell out.

In her free hand is a silver flask. It explains a lot.

She tilts her head. "First person picks someone and dares them to do something. Then that person has a drink, does the dare, and gets a chance to dare someone else to do something. And when everyone has done their dare—or died trying—we get a little drunk and stumble home."

"How do you win?" one of the Dauntless calls out from the other side of the train car. A boy who sits slouched against Amar like they're old friends, or brothers.

I'm not the only initiate in the train car. Sitting across from me is Zeke, the first jumper, and a girl with brown hair and bangs cut straight across her forehead, and a pierced lip. The others are older, Dauntless members all. They have a kind of ease with one another, leaning into one another, punching one another's arms, tousling one another's hair. It's camaraderie and friendship and flirtation, and none of it is familiar to me. I try to relax, bending my arms around my knees.

I really am a Stiff.

"You win by not being a little pansycake," Lauren says. "And, hey, new rule, you also win by not asking dumb questions.

"I'm gonna go first, as the keeper of the alcohol," she adds. "Amar, I dare you to go into the Erudite library while all the Noses are studying and scream something obscene."

She screws the cap on the flask and tosses it to him. Everyone cheers as Amar takes the cap off and takes a swallow of whatever liquor is inside.

"Just tell me when we get to the right stop!" he shouts over the cheering.

Zeke waves a hand at me. "Hey, you're a transfer, right? Four?"

"Yeah," I say. "Nice first jump."

I realize, too late, that it might be a sore spot for him—his moment of triumph, stolen by a misstep and loss of balance. But he just laughs.

"Yeah, not my finest moment," he says.

"Not like anyone else stepped up," the girl at his side says. "I'm Shauna, by the way. Is it true you only had four fears?"

"Hence the name," I say.

"Wow." She nods. She looks impressed, which makes me sit up straighter. "Guess you were born Dauntless."

I shrug, like what she says might be true, even though I'm sure it's not. She doesn't know that I came here to escape the life I was meant for, that I'm fighting so hard to get through initiation so I don't have to admit that I'm an imposter. Abnegation-born, Abnegation result, in a Dauntless haven.

The corners of her mouth turn down, like she's sad about something, but I don't ask what it is.

"How are your fights going?" Zeke asks me.

"All right," I say. I wave a hand over my bruised face. "As you can clearly tell."

"Check it out." Zeke turns his head, showing me a large bruise on the underside of his jaw. "That's thanks to this girl over here."

He indicates Shauna with his thumb.

"He beat me," Shauna says. "But I got a good shot in, for once. I keep losing."

"It doesn't bother you that he hit you?" I say.

"Why would it?" she says.

"I don't know," I say. "Because . . . you're a girl?"

She raises her eyebrows. "What, you think I can't take it just like every other initiate, just because I have girl parts?" She gestures to her chest, and I catch myself staring, just for a second, before I remember to look away, my face flushing.

"Sorry," I say. "I didn't mean it that way. I'm just not used to this. Any of it."

"Sure, I get it," she says, and she doesn't sound angry. "But you should know that about Dauntless—girl, guy, whatever, it doesn't matter here. What matters is what you've got in your gut."

Then Amar gets up, putting his hands on his hips in a dramatic stance, and marches toward the open doorway. The train dips down and Amar doesn't even hold on to anything, he just shifts and sways with the car's movement. Everyone gets up, and Amar is the first one to jump, launching himself into the night. The others stream out behind him, and I let the people behind me carry me toward the opening. I'm not afraid of the speed of the train, just the heights, but here the train is close to the ground, so when I jump, I do it without fear. I land on two feet, stumbling for a few steps before I stop.

"Look at you, getting your train legs," Amar says, elbowing me. "Here, have a sip. You look like you need it."

He holds out the flask.

I've never tasted alcohol. The Abnegation don't drink it, so it wasn't even available. But I've seen how comfortable it seems to make people, and I desperately want to feel like I'm not wrapped up in skin that's too tight for me to wear, so I don't hesitate: I take the flask and drink.

The alcohol burns and tastes like medicine, but it goes down fast, leaving me warm.

"Good job," Amar says, and he moves on to Zeke, hooking his arm around Zeke's neck and dragging Zeke's head against his chest. "I see you've met my young friend Ezekiel."

"Just because my mom calls me that doesn't mean you have to," Zeke says, throwing Amar off. He looks at me. "Amar's grandparents were friends with my parents."

"Were?"

"Well, my dad's dead, and so are the grandparents," Zeke says.

"What about your parents?" I ask Amar.

He shrugs. "Died when I was young. Train accident. Very sad." He grins like it's not. "And my grandparents took the jump after I became an official member of Dauntless." He makes a careening gesture with his hand, suggesting a dive.

"The jump?"

"Oh, don't tell him while I'm here," Zeke says, shaking his head. "I don't want to see the look on his face."

Amar doesn't pay attention. "Elderly Dauntless sometimes take a flying leap into the unknown of the chasm when they hit a certain age. It's that or be factionless," Amar says. "And my grandpa was really sick. Cancer. Grandma didn't care to go on without him."

He tilts his head up to the sky, and his eyes reflect the moonlight. For a moment I feel like he is showing me a secret self, one carefully hidden beneath layers of charm and humor and Dauntless bravado, and it scares me, because that secret self is hard, and cold, and sad.

"I'm sorry," I say.

"At least this way, I got to say my good-byes," Amar says. "Most of the time death just comes whether you've said good-bye or not."

The secret self vanishes with the flash of a smile, and Amar jogs toward the rest of the group, flask in hand. I stay back with Zeke. He lopes along, somehow clumsy and graceful at once, like a wild dog.

"What about you?" Zeke says. "You have parents?"

"One," I say. "My mother died a long time ago."

I remember the funeral, with all the Abnegation filling our house with quiet chatter, staying with us in our grief. They carried us meals on metal trays, covered with tinfoil, and cleaned our kitchen, and boxed up all my mother's clothes for us, so there were no traces of her left. I remember them murmuring that she died from complications with another child. But I had a memory of her, a few months before her death, standing in front of her dresser, buttoning up her loose second shirt over the tight undershirt, her stomach flat. I shake my head a little, banishing the memory. She's dead. It's a child's memory, unreliable.

"And your dad, is he okay with your choice?" he says. "Visiting Day is coming up, you know."

"No," I say distantly. "He's not okay with it at all."

My father will not come on Visiting Day. I'm sure of it. He will never speak to me again.

The Erudite sector is cleaner than any other part of the city, every scrap of trash or rubble cleared from the pavement, every crack in the street shored up with tar. I feel like I need to step carefully rather than mar the sidewalk with my sneakers. The other Dauntless walk along carelessly, the soles of their shoes making slapping sounds like pattering rain.

Every faction headquarters is allowed to have the lights on in its lobby at midnight, but everything else is supposed to be dark. Here, in the Erudite sector, each building that makes up Erudite headquarters is like a pillar of light. The windows we walk past feature the Erudite sitting at long tables, their noses buried in books or screens, or talking quietly to one another. The young and the old mix together at every table, in their impeccable blue clothing, their smooth hair, more than half of them with gleaming spectacles. *Vanity,* my father would say. *They are so concerned with looking intelligent that they make themselves fools for it.*

I pause to watch them. They don't look vain to me. They look like people who make every effort to feel as smart as they are supposed to be. If that means wearing glasses with no prescription, it isn't my place to judge. They are a haven I might have chosen. Instead I chose the haven that mocks them through the windows, that sends Amar into their lobby to cause a stir.

Amar reaches the doors of the central Erudite building and pushes through them. We watch from just outside, snickering. I peer through the doors at the portrait of Jeanine Matthews hanging on the opposite wall. Her yellow hair is pulled back tight from her face, her blue jacket buttoned just beneath her throat. She's pretty, but that's not the first thing I notice about her. Her sharpness is.

And beyond that—it could just be my imagination, but does she look a little afraid?

Amar runs into the lobby, ignoring the protests of the Erudite at the front desk, and yells, "Hey, Noses! Check this out!"

All the Erudite in the lobby look up from their books or screens, and the Dauntless burst into laughter as Amar turns, mooning them. The Erudite behind the desk run around it to catch him, but Amar pulls up his pants and runs toward us. We all start running, too, sprinting away from the doors.

I can't help it—I'm laughing too, and it surprises me, how my stomach aches with it. Zeke runs at my shoulder, and we go toward the train tracks because there's nowhere else to run. The Erudite chasing us give up after a block, and we all stop in an alley, leaning against the brick to catch our breath.

Amar comes into the alley last, his hands raised, and we cheer for him. He holds up the flask like it's a trophy and points at Shauna.

"Young one," he says. "I dare you to scale the sculpture in front of the Upper Levels building."

She catches the flask when he throws it and takes a swig.

"You got it," she says, grinning.

+ + +

By the time they get to me, almost everyone is drunk, lurching with each footstep and laughing at every joke, no matter how stupid it is. I feel warm, despite the cool air, but my mind is still sharp, taking in everything about the night, the rich smell of marsh and the sound of bubbling laughter, the blue-black of the sky and the silhouette of each building against it. My legs are sore from running and walking and climbing, and still I haven't fulfilled a dare.

We're close to Dauntless headquarters now. The buildings are sagging where they stand.

"Who's left?" Lauren says, her bleary eyes skipping over each face until she reaches mine. "Ah, the numerically named initiate from Abnegation. Four, is it?"

"Yeah," I say.

"A Stiff?" The boy who sat so comfortably beside Amar looks at me, his words running together. He's the one holding the flask, the one determining the next dare. So far I've watched people scale tall structures, I've watched them jump into dark holes and wander into empty buildings to retrieve a faucet or a desk chair, I've watched them run naked down alleyways and stick needles through their earlobes without numbing them first. If I was asked to concoct a dare, I would not be able to think of one. It's a good thing I'm the last person to go.

I feel a tremor in my chest, nerves. What will he tell me to do?

"Stiffs are uptight," the boy says plainly, like it's a fact. "So, to prove you're really Dauntless now . . . I dare you to get a tattoo."

I see their ink, creeping over wrists and arms and shoulders and throats. The metal studs through ears and noses and lips and eyebrows. My skin is blank, healed, whole. But it doesn't match who I am—I should be scarred, marked, the way they are, but marked with memories of pain, scarred with the things I have survived.

I lift a shoulder. "Fine."

He tosses me the flask, and I drain it, though it stings my throat and lips and tastes bitter as poison.

We start toward the Pire.

+ + +

Tori is wearing a pair of men's underwear and a T-shirt when she answers the door, her hair hanging over the left half of her face. She raises an eyebrow at me. We clearly woke her from a sound sleep, but she doesn't seem angry— just a little grouchy.

"Please?" Amar says. "It's for a game of Dare."

"Are you sure you want a tired woman to tattoo your

skin, Four? This ink doesn't wash off," she says to me.

"I trust you," I say. I'm not going to back out of the dare, not after watching everyone else do theirs.

"Right." Tori yawns. "The things I do for Dauntless tradition. I'll be right back, I'm going to put on pants."

She closes the door between us. On the way here I racked my brain for what I might want tattooed, and where. I couldn't decide—my thoughts were too muddled. Still are.

A few seconds later Tori emerges wearing pants, her feet still bare. "If I get in trouble for turning on lights at this hour, I'm going to claim it was vandals and name names."

"Got it," I say.

"There's a back way. Come on," she says, beckoning to us. I follow her through her dark living room, which is tidy except for the sheets of paper spread over her coffee table, each one marked with a different drawing. Some of them are harsh and simple, like most of the tattoos I've seen, and others are more intricate, detailed. Tori must be the Dauntless approximation of an artist.

I pause by the table. One of the pages depicts all the faction symbols, without the circles that usually bind them. The Amity tree is at the bottom, forming a kind of root system for the eye of Erudite and the Candor scales. Above them, the Abnegation hands seem almost to cradle the Dauntless flames. It's like the symbols are growing into one another.

The others have moved past me. I jog to catch up, walking through Tori's kitchen—also immaculate, though the appliances are out of date, the faucet rusted, and the refrigerator door held closed by a large clamp. The back door is open and leads into a short, dank hallway that opens up to the tattoo parlor.

I've walked past it before but never cared to go inside, sure I wasn't going to find a reason to attack my own body with needles. I guess I have one now—those needles are a way for me to separate myself from my past, not just in the eyes of my fellow Dauntless, but in my own eyes, every time I look at my own reflection.

The room's walls are covered in pictures. The wall by the door is entirely dedicated to Dauntless symbols, some black and simple, some colorful and barely recognizable. Tori turns on the light over one of the chairs and arranges her tattoo needles on a tray next to it. The other Dauntless gather on benches and chairs around us, like they're getting ready to see a performance of some kind. My face gets hot.

"Basic principles of tattooing," Tori says. "The less cushion under the skin, or the bonier you are in a particular area, the more painful the tattoo. For your first one it's probably best to get it done on, I don't know, your arm, or—"

"Your butt cheek," Zeke suggests, with a snort of laughter.

Tori shrugs. "It wouldn't be the first time. Or the last."

I look at the boy who dared me. He raises his eyebrows at me. I know what he expects, what they all expect—that I'll get something small, on an arm or a leg, something that's easily hidden. I glance at the wall with all the symbols. One of the drawings in particular catches my eye, an artistic rendering of the flames themselves.

"That one," I say, pointing to it.

"Got it," Tori says. "Got a location in mind?"

I have a scar—a faint gouge in my knee from when I fell down on the sidewalk as a child. It's always seemed stupid to me that none of the pain I've experienced has left a visible mark; sometimes, without a way to prove it to myself, I began to doubt that I had lived through it at all, with the memories becoming hazy over time. I want to have some kind of reminder that while wounds heal, they don't disappear forever—I carry them everywhere, always, and that is the way of things, the way of scars.

That is what this tattoo will be, for me: a scar. And it seems fitting that it should document the worst memory of pain that I have.

I rest my hand on my rib cage, remembering the bruises that were, and the fear I felt for my own life. My father had a series of bad nights right after my mother died.

"You sure?" Tori says. "That's maybe the most painful place possible."

"Good," I say, and I sit down in the chair.

The crowd of Dauntless cheer and start passing around another flask, this one bigger than the last, and bronze instead of silver.

"So we have a masochist in the chair tonight. Lovely." Tori sits on the stool next to me and puts on a pair of rubber gloves. I sit forward, lifting up the hem of my shirt, and she soaks a cotton ball in rubbing alcohol, covering my ribs with it. She's about to move away when she frowns and pulls at my skin with her fingertip. Rubbing alcohol bites into the still-healing skin of my back, and I wince.

"How did this happen, Four?" she asks.

I look up and notice that Amar is staring at me, frowning.

"He's an initiate," Amar says. "They're *all* cut and bruised at this point. You should see them all limping around together. It's sad."

"I have a giant one on my knee," volunteers Zeke. "It's the sickest blue color—"

Zeke rolls up his pant leg to display his bruise to the others, and they all start sharing their own bruises, their own scars: "Got this when they *dropped* me after the zip line." "Well, I've got a stab wound from your grip slipping during knife-throwing, so I think we're even." Tori eyes me for a few seconds, and I'm sure she doesn't accept Amar's explanation for the marks on my back, but she doesn't ask again. Instead, she turns on the needle, filling the air with the sound of buzzing, and Amar tosses me the flask.

The alcohol is still burning my throat when the tattoo needle touches my ribs, and I wince, but somehow I don't mind the pain.

I relish it.

+++

The next day, when I wake up, everything hurts. Especially my head.

Oh God, my head.

Eric is perched on the edge of the mattress next to mine, tying his shoelaces. The skin around the rings in his lip looks red—he must have pierced it recently. I haven't been paying attention.

He looks at me. "You look like hell."

I sit up, and the sudden motion makes my head throb more.

"I hope that when you lose, you don't use it as an excuse," he says, sneering a little. "Because I would have beat you anyway."

He gets up, stretches, and leaves the dormitory. I cradle my head in my hands for a few seconds, then get up to take a shower. I have to stand with half my body under the water and half out, because of the ink on my side. The Dauntless stayed with me for hours, waiting for the tattoo to be finished, and by the time we left, all the flasks were empty. Tori gave me a thumbs-up as I stumbled out of the tattoo parlor, and Zeke slung an arm across my shoulders and said, "I think you're Dauntless now."

Last night I found myself relishing the words. Now I wish I could have my old head back, the one that was focused and determined and didn't feel like tiny men with hammers had taken up residence inside it. I let the cool water spill over me for a few more minutes, then check the clock on the bathroom wall.

Ten minutes to the fight. I'm going to be late. And Eric is right—I'm going to lose.

I push my hand into my forehead as I run toward the training room, my feet halfway out of my shoes. When I burst through the doors, the transfer initiates and some of the Dauntless-born initiates are standing around the edge of the room. Amar is in the center of the arena, checking his watch. He gives me a pointed look.

"Nice of you to join us," he says. I see in his raised eyebrows that the camaraderie of the night before does not extend to the training room. He points at my shoes. "Tie your shoes, and don't waste any more of my time."

Across the arena, Eric cracks each one of his knuckles, carefully, staring at me the whole time. I tie my shoes in a hurry and tuck the ends of the laces under so they don't get in my way.

As I face Eric I can feel only the pounding of my heart, the throbbing of my head, the burning in my side. Then Amar steps back, and Eric rushes forward, fast, his fist hitting me square in the jaw.

I stumble back, holding my face. All the pain runs together in my mind. I put up my hands to block the next punch. My head throbs and I see his leg move. I try to twist away from the kick, but his foot hits me hard in the ribs. I feel a sensation like an electric shock through the left side of my body.

"This is easier than I thought it would be," Eric says.

I feel hot with embarrassment, and in the arrogant opening he leaves me, I uppercut him in the stomach.

The flat of his hand smacks into my ear, making it ring, and I lose my balance, my fingers touching the ground to steady me.

"You know," Eric says quietly, "I think I've figured out your real name."

My eyes are blurry with half a dozen different kinds of pain. I didn't know it came in so many varieties, like flavors, acid and fire and ache and sting.

He hits me again, this time trying for my face but getting my collarbone instead. He shakes out his hand and says, "Should I tell them? Get everything out in the open?"

He has my name between his teeth, *Eaton*, a far more threatening weapon than his feet or his elbows or his fists. The Abnegation say, in hushed voices, that the problem with many Erudite is their selfishness, but I think it is their arrogance, the pride they take in knowing things that others do not. In that moment, overwhelmed with fear, I recognize it as Eric's weakness. He doesn't believe that I can hurt him as much as he can hurt me. He believes that I am everything he assumed me to be at the outset, humble and selfless and passive.

I feel my pain disappear into rage, and I grab his arm to hold him in place as I swing at him again, and again, and again. I don't even see where I'm hitting him; I don't see or feel or hear anything. I am empty, alone, nothing.

Then I finally hear his screams, see him clutching his face with both hands. Blood soaks his chin, runs into his teeth. He tries to wrench away but I am holding on as hard as I can, holding on for dear life.

I kick him hard in the side, so he topples. Over his clutched hands, I meet his eyes.

His eyes are glassy and unfocused. His blood is bright against his skin. It occurs to me that I did that, it was me, and fear creeps back in, a different kind of fear this time. A fear of what I am, what I might be becoming.

My knuckles throb, and I walk out of the arena without being dismissed.

+ + +

The Dauntless compound is a good place to recover, dark and full of secret, quiet places.

I find a hallway near the Pit and sit against the wall, letting the cold from the stone seep into me. My headache has returned, as well as various aches and pains from the fight, but I barely register any of them. My knuckles are tacky with blood, Eric's. I try to rub it off but it's been drying too long. I won the fight, and that means my place in Dauntless is secure for the time being—I should feel satisfied, not afraid. Maybe even happy, to finally belong somewhere, to be among people whose eyes don't skirt mine at the lunch table. But I know that for every good thing that comes along, there is always a cost. What is the cost of being Dauntless?

"Hey." I look up and see Shauna knocking on the stone

wall like it's a door. She grins. "This is not quite the victory dance I was expecting."

"I don't dance," I say.

"Yeah, I should have known better." She sits across from me, her back against the opposite wall. She draws her knees up to her chest and wraps her arms around them. Our feet are just a few inches apart. I don't know why I notice that. Well, yes I do—she's a girl.

I don't know how to talk to girls. Especially not a Dauntless girl. Something tells me you can never know what to expect from a Dauntless girl.

"Eric's in the hospital," she says, and there's a grin on her face. "They think you broke his nose. You definitely knocked out one of his teeth."

I look down. I knocked out someone's tooth?

"I was wondering if you could help me," she says, nudging my shoe with her toe.

As I suspected: Dauntless girls are unpredictable. "Help you with what?"

"Fighting. I'm no good at it. I keep getting humiliated in the arena." She shakes her head. "I have to face off with this girl in two days, her name's Ashley but she makes everyone call her Ash." Shauna rolls her eyes. "You know, Dauntless flames, ash, whatever. Anyway, she's one of the best people in our group, and I'm afraid she's going to kill me. Like actually kill me."

"Why do you want my help?" I say, suddenly suspicious. "Because you know I'm a Stiff and we're supposed to help people?"

"What? No, of course not," she says. Her eyebrows furrow in confusion. "I want your help because you're the best in *your* group, obviously."

I laugh. "No, I'm not."

"You and Eric were the only undefeated ones and you just beat him, so yeah, you are. Listen, if you don't want to help me, all you have to do is—"

"I'll help," I say. "I just don't really know how."

"We'll figure it out," she says. "Tomorrow afternoon? Meet you in the arena?"

I nod. She grins, gets up, and starts to leave. But a few steps away and she turns around, moving backward down the hallway.

"Quit sulking, Four," she says. "Everyone's impressed with you. Embrace it."

I watch her silhouette turn the corner at the end of the hallway. I was so disturbed by the fight that I never thought about what beating Eric meant—that I am now first in my initiate class. I may have chosen Dauntless as a haven, but I'm not just surviving here, I'm excelling.

I stare at Eric's blood on my knuckles and smile.

+ + +

The next morning I decide to take a risk. I sit with Zeke and Shauna at breakfast. Shauna mostly just slumps over her food and answers questions in grunts. Zeke yawns into his coffee, but he points out his family to me: his little brother, Uriah, sits at one of the other tables with Lynn, Shauna's little sister. His mother, Hana—the tamest Dauntless I've ever seen, her faction indicated only by the color of her clothing—is still in the breakfast line.

"Do you miss living at home?" I say.

The Dauntless have a proclivity for baked goods, I've noticed. There are always at least two different kinds of cake at dinner, and a mountain of muffins rests on a table near the end of the breakfast line. When I got there, all the good flavors were gone, so I was left with bran.

"Not really," he says. "I mean, they're right there. Dauntless-born initiates aren't really supposed to talk to family until Visiting Day, but I know if I really needed something, they'd be there."

I nod. Beside him, Shauna's eyes close, and she falls asleep with her chin resting on her hand.

"What about you?" he says. "Do you miss home?"

I am about to answer no, but right at that moment Shauna's chin slips off her hand and she smashes her chocolate muffin with her face. Zeke laughs so hard he cries, and I can't help but grin as I finish my juice.

+++

Later that morning I meet Shauna in the training room. She has her short hair pulled back from her face, and her Dauntless boots, normally untied and flapping when she walks, laced up tight. She's punching at nothing, pausing between each hit to adjust her position, and for a moment I watch her, not sure how to start. I only just learned to throw a punch myself; I'm hardly qualified to teach her anything.

But as I watch her, I start to notice things. How she stands with her knees locked, how she doesn't hold up a hand to protect her jaw, how she punches from her elbow instead of throwing her body weight behind each hit. She stops, wiping her forehead with the back of her hand. When she notices me, she jumps like she just touched a live wire.

"Rule number one for not being creepy," she says. "Announce your presence in a room if another person doesn't see you come in."

"Sorry," I say. "I was coming up with some pointers for you."

"Oh." She chews on the inside of her cheek. "What are they?"

I tell her what I noticed, and then we face off in the

fighting arena. We begin slowly, pulling back on each hit so we don't hurt each other. I have to keep tapping her elbow with my fist to remind her to keep her hand up by her face, but a half hour later, she's at least moving better than she was before.

"This girl you have to fight tomorrow," I say. "I'd get her right here, in the jaw." I touch the underside of my jaw. "A good uppercut should do it. Let's practice those."

She squares off, and I notice with satisfaction that her knees are bent, and there's a bounce in her stance that wasn't there before. We shuffle around each other for a few seconds, and then she punches up. As she does, her left hand drops from her face. I block the first punch, then start to attack the hole she left in her guard. At the last second, I stop my fist in the air and raise my eyebrows at her.

"You know, maybe I would learn my lesson if you actually hit me," she says, straightening. Her skin is flushed from exertion, and sweat shines along her hairline. Her eyes are bright and critical. It occurs to me, for the first time, that she's pretty. Not in the way I usually think of—she's not soft, delicate—but in a way that's strong, capable.

I say, "I would really rather not."

"What you think is some kind of lingering Abnegation chivalry is really kind of insulting," she says. "I can take care of myself. I can take a little pain."

"It's not that," I say. "It's not because you're a girl. I just . . . I'm not really into violence for no reason."

"Some kind of Stiff thing, huh?" she says.

"Not really. Stiffs aren't into violence, period. Put a Stiff in Dauntless and they just let themselves get punched a lot," I say, letting myself smile a little. I'm not used to using Dauntless slang, but it feels good to claim it as my own, to let myself relax into their rhythms of speech. "It just doesn't feel like a game to me, that's all."

It's the first time I've expressed that to anyone. I know why it doesn't feel like a game—because for so long, it was my reality, it was my waking and my sleeping. Here, I've learned to defend myself, I've learned to be stronger, but one thing I haven't learned, won't let myself learn, is how to enjoy causing someone else pain. If I'm going to become Dauntless, I'm going to do it on my terms, even if that means that a part of me will always be a Stiff.

"All right," she says. "Let's go again."

We spar until she's mastered the uppercut and we've almost missed dinner. When we leave, she thanks me, and casually, she wraps an arm around me. It's just a quick embrace, but she laughs at how tense it makes me.

"How to Be Dauntless: An Introductory Course," she says. "Lesson one: It's okay to hug your friends here."

"We're friends?" I say, only halfway joking.

"Oh, shut up," she says, and she jogs down the hallway toward the dormitory.

+ + +

The next morning, all the transfer initiates follow Amar past the training room to a grim hallway with a heavy door at the end of it. He tells us to sit against the wall, and then disappears behind the door without saying anything. I check my watch. Shauna will be fighting any minute now—it's taking the Dauntless-borns longer to get through the first phase of initiation than us, since there are more of them.

Eric sits as far away from me as he can, and I am glad for the distance. The night after I fought him, it occurred to me that he might tell everyone that I'm Marcus Eaton's son just to spite me for beating him, but he hasn't done it. I wonder if he's just waiting for the right opportunity to strike, or if he's holding back for another reason. No matter what, it's probably better for me to stay away from him as much as possible.

"What do you think is in there?" Mia, the Amity transfer, sounds nervous.

No one answers. For some reason I don't feel nervous. There's nothing behind that door that can hurt me. So when Amar steps into the hallway again and calls my name first, I don't cast desperate looks at my fellow initiates. I just follow him in.

The room is dim and grungy, with just a chair and a computer in it. The chair is reclined, like the one I sat in for my aptitude test. The computer screen is bright and running a program that amounts to lines of dark text on a white background. When I was younger, I used to volunteer at the school in the computer labs, maintaining the facilities, and sometimes even fixing the computers themselves when they failed. I worked under the supervision of an Erudite woman named Katherine, and she taught me far more than she had to, happy to share her knowledge with someone who was willing to listen. So I know, looking at that code, what kind of program I'm looking at, though I would never be able to do much with it.

"A simulation?" I say.

"The less you know, the better," he says. "Sit down."

I sit, leaning back in the chair and setting my arms on the armrests. Amar prepares a syringe, holding it up to the light to make sure the vial is locked in place. He sticks the needle into my neck without warning and presses down on the plunger. I flinch.

"Let's see which of your four fears comes up first," he

says. "You know, I'm getting kind of bored of them, you might try to show me something new."

"I'll work on it," I say.

The simulation swallows me.

+ + +

I am sitting on the hard wooden bench at an Abnegation kitchen table, an empty plate in front of me. All the shades are drawn over the windows, so the only light comes from the bulb dangling over the table, its filament glowing orange. I stare at the dark fabric covering my knee. *Why am I wearing black instead of gray?*

When I lift my head, he—Marcus—is across from me. For a split second, he's just like the man I saw across the Choosing Ceremony hall not long ago, his eyes dark blue to match mine, his mouth pressed into a frown.

I'm wearing black because I'm Dauntless now, I remind myself. *So why am I in an Abnegation house, sitting across from my father?*

I see the outline of the lightbulb reflected in my empty plate. *This must be a simulation,* I think.

Then the light above us flickers, and he turns into the man I always see in my fear landscape, a twisted monster with pits for eyes and a wide, empty mouth. He lunges across the table with both hands outstretched, and instead of fingernails he has razor blades embedded in his fingertips.

He swipes at me, and I lurch back, falling off the bench. I scramble on the floor for my balance, then run into the living room. There is another Marcus there, reaching for me from the wall. I search for the front door, but someone has sealed it with cinder blocks, trapping me.

Gasping, I sprint up the stairs. At the top I trip, and sprawl on the wooden floor in the hallway. A Marcus opens the closet door from the inside; another one walks out of my parents' bedroom; yet another one claws across the floor from the bathroom. I shrink back against the wall. The house is dark. There are no windows.

This place is full of him.

Suddenly one of the Marcuses is right in front of me, pressing me to the wall with both hands around my throat. Another one drags his fingernails down my arms, provoking a stinging pain that brings tears to my eyes.

I am paralyzed, panicking.

I swallow air. I can't scream. I feel pain and my pounding heart and I kick as hard as I can, hitting only air. The Marcus with his hands around my throat shoves me up the wall, so my toes drag along the floor. My limbs are limp, like a rag doll's. I can't move.

This place, this place is full of him. *It's not real,* I realize.

It's a simulation. It's just like the fear landscape.

There are more Marcuses now, waiting below me with their hands outstretched, so I'm staring down at a sea of blades. Their fingers clutch at my legs, cutting me, and I feel a hot trail down the side of my neck as the Marcus who is choking me digs in harder.

Simulation, I remind myself. I try to send life into every one of my limbs. I imagine my blood on fire, racing through me. I slap my hand against the wall, searching for a weapon. One of the Marcuses reaches up, his fingers poised over my eyes. I scream and thrash as the blades dig into my eyelids.

My hands find not a weapon but a doorknob. I twist it, hard, and fall back into another closet. The Marcuses lose their hold on me. In the closet is a window, just big enough for my body. As they chase me into the darkness, I throw my shoulder against the glass, and it shatters. Fresh air fills my lungs.

I sit upright in the chair, gasping.

I put my hands against my throat, on my arms, on my legs, checking for wounds that aren't there. I can still feel the cuts and the unfurling of blood from my veins, but my skin is intact.

My breaths slow down, and with them, my thoughts.

Amar is sitting at the computer, hooked up to the simulation, and he's staring at me.

"What?" I say, breathless.

"You were in there for five minutes," Amar says.

"Is that long?"

"No." He frowns at me. "No, it's not long at all. It's very good, actually."

I put my feet on the floor and hold my head in my hands. I may not have panicked for that long during the simulation, but the image of my warped father trying to claw my eyes out keeps flashing in my mind, causing my heart rate to spike again and again.

"Is the serum still in effect?" I say, clenching my teeth. "Making me panic?"

"No, it should have gone dormant when you exited the simulation," he says. "Why?"

I shake my hands, which are tingling, like they're going numb. I shake my head. *It wasn't real,* I tell myself. *Let it go.*

"Sometimes the simulation causes lingering panic, depending on what you see in it," Amar says. "Let me walk you back to the dormitory."

"No." I shake my head. "I'll be fine."

He gives me a hard look.

"It wasn't a request," he says. He gets up and opens a

door behind the chair. I follow him down a short, dark hallway and into the stone corridors that lead back to the transfer dormitory. The air is cool there, and moist, from being underground. I hear our footsteps echo, and my own breaths, but nothing else.

I think I see something—movement—on my left, and I flinch away from it, pulling back against the wall. Amar stops me, putting his hands on my shoulders so I have to look at his face.

"Hey," he says. "Get it together, Four."

I nod, heat rushing into my face. I feel a deep twinge of shame in my stomach. I am supposed to be Dauntless. I am not supposed to be afraid of monster Marcuses creeping up on me in the dark. I lean against the stone wall and take a deep breath.

"Can I ask you something?" Amar says. I cringe, thinking he's going to ask me about my father, but he doesn't. "How did you get out of that hallway?"

"I opened a door," I say.

"Was there a door behind you the whole time? Is there one in your old house?"

I shake my head.

Amar's usually amiable face is serious. "So you created one out of nowhere?"

"Yeah," I say. "Simulations are all in your head. So my

head made a door so I could get out. All I had to do was concentrate."

"Strange," he says.

"What? Why?"

"Most initiates can't make something impossible happen in these simulations, because unlike in the fear landscape, they don't recognize that they are *in* a simulation," he says. "And they don't get out of simulations that fast, as a result."

I feel my pulse in my throat. I didn't realize these simulations were supposed to be different from the fear landscape—I thought everyone was aware of this simulation while they were in it. But judging by what Amar is saying, this was supposed to be like the aptitude test, and before the aptitude test, my father warned me against my simulation awareness, coached me to hide it. I still remember how insistent he was, how tense his voice was and how he grabbed my arm a little too hard.

At the time, I thought that he would never speak that way unless he was worried about me. Worried for my safety.

Was he just being paranoid, or is there still something dangerous about being aware during simulations?

"I was like you," Amar says quietly. "I could change the simulations. I just thought I was the only one."

I want to tell him to keep it to himself, to protect his secrets. But the Dauntless don't care about secrets the way the Abnegation do, with their tight-lipped smiles and identical, orderly houses.

Amar is giving me a strange look—eager, like he expects something from me. I shift, uncomfortable.

"It's probably not something you should brag about," Amar says. "The Dauntless are all about conformity, just like every other faction. It's just not as obvious here."

I nod.

"It's probably just a fluke," I say. "I couldn't do that during my aptitude test. Next time I'll probably be more normal."

"Right." He doesn't sound convinced. "Well, next time, try not to do anything impossible, all right? Just face your fear in a logical way, a way that would always make sense to you whether you were aware or not."

"Okay," I say.

"You're okay now, right? You can get back to the dorms on your own?"

I want to say that I could always get back to the dormitory on my own; I never needed him to take me there. But I just nod again. He claps me on the shoulder, good-naturedly, and walks back to the simulation room.

I can't help but think that my father wouldn't have

warned me against displaying my simulation awareness just because of faction norms. He scolded me for embarrassing him in front of the Abnegation all the time, but he had never hissed warnings in my ears or taught me how to avoid a misstep before. He never stared at me, wide-eyed, until I promised to do as he said.

It feels strange, to know that he must have been trying to protect me. Like he's not quite the monster I imagine, the one I see in my worst nightmares.

As I start toward the dorms, I hear something at the end of the hallway we just walked down—something like quiet, shuffling footsteps, moving in the opposite direction.

+ + +

Shauna runs up to me in the cafeteria at dinner and punches me hard in the arm. She's wearing a smile so wide it looks like it's cutting into her cheeks. There's some swelling just beneath her right eye—she'll have a black eye later.

"I won!" she says. "I did what you said—got her right in the jaw within the first sixty seconds, and it totally threw her off her game. She still hit me in the eye because I let my guard down, but after that I pummeled her. She has a bloody nose. It was awesome."

I grin. I'm surprised by how satisfying it is, to teach

someone how to do something and then to hear that it actually worked.

"Well done," I say.

"I couldn't have done it without your help," she says. Her smile changes, softens, less giddy and more sincere. She stands on her tiptoes and kisses my cheek.

I stare at her as she pulls away. She laughs and drags me toward the table where Zeke and some of the other Dauntless-born initiates sit. My problem, I realize, isn't that I'm a Stiff, it's that I don't know what these gestures of affection mean to the Dauntless. Shauna is pretty, and funny, and in Abnegation I would go over to her house for dinner with her family if I was interested in her, I would find out what volunteering project she was working on and insinuate myself into it. In Dauntless I have no idea how to go about that, or how to know if I even like her that way.

I decide not to let it distract me, at least not now. I get a plate of food and sit down to eat it, listening to the others talk and laugh together. Everyone congratulates Shauna on her win, and they point out the girl she beat up, sitting at one of the other tables, her face still swollen. At the end of the meal, when I'm poking at a piece of chocolate cake with my fork, a pair of Erudite women walk into the room.

It takes a lot to make the Dauntless go quiet. Even the sudden appearance of the Erudite doesn't quite do it—there are still mutters everywhere, like the distant sound of running footsteps. But gradually, as the Erudite sit down with Max and nothing else happens, conversations pick up again. I don't participate in them. I keep stabbing the cake with the fork tines, watching.

Max stands and approaches Amar. They have a tense conversation between the tables, and then they start walking in my direction. Toward *me*.

Amar beckons to me. I leave my almost-empty tray behind.

"You and I have been called in for an evaluation," Amar says. His perpetually smiling mouth is now a flat line, his animated voice a monotone.

"Evaluation?" I say.

Max smiles at me, a little. "Your fear simulation results were a little abnormal. Our Erudite friends behind us—" I look over his shoulder at the Erudite women. With a start, I realize that one of them is Jeanine Matthews, representative of Erudite. She's dressed in a crisp blue suit, with a pair of spectacles dangling from a chain around her neck, a symbol of Erudite vanity pushed so far as to be illogical. Max continues, "Will observe another simulation to make sure that the abnormal result wasn't an error in the simulation program. Amar will take you all to the fear simulation room now."

I feel my father's fingers clamped around my arm, hear his hissing voice, warning me not to do anything strange in my aptitude test simulation. I feel tingling in my palms, the sign that I'm about to panic. I can't speak, so I just look at Max, and then at Amar, and nod. I don't know what it means, to be aware during a simulation, but I know it can't be good. I know that Jeanine Matthews would never come here just to observe my simulation if something wasn't seriously wrong with me.

We walk to the fear simulation room without speaking, Jeanine and her assistant—I'm assuming—talking quietly behind us. Amar opens the door and lets us file in.

"I'll go get the extra equipment so you can observe," Amar says. "Be right back."

Jeanine paces around the room with a thoughtful expression. I'm wary of her, as all Abnegation are, taught to distrust Erudite vanity, Erudite greed. It occurs to me, though, as I watch her, that what I was taught might not be right. The Erudite woman who taught me how to take apart a computer when I was volunteering in the computer labs at school wasn't greedy or vain; maybe Jeanine Matthews isn't, either.

"You were logged into the system as 'Four,'" Jeanine says after a few seconds. She stops pacing, folding her hands in front of her. "Which I found perplexing. Why do you not go by 'Tobias' here?"

She already knows who I am. Well, of course she does. She knows everything, doesn't she? I feel like my insides are shriveling up, collapsing into each other. She knows my name, she knows my father, and if she's seen one of my fear simulations, she knows some of the darkest parts of me, too. Her clear, almost watery eyes touch mine, and I look away.

"I wanted a clean slate," I say.

She nods. "I can appreciate that. Especially given what you've gone through."

She sounds almost . . . *gentle*. I bristle at her tone, staring her straight in the face. "I'm fine," I say coldly.

"Of course you are." She smiles a little.

Amar wheels a cart into the room. It carries more wires, electrodes, computer parts. I know what I'm supposed to do; I sit down in the reclining chair and put my arms on the armrests as the others hook themselves up to the simulation. Amar approaches me with a needle, and I stay still as it pinches my throat.

I close my eyes, and the world falls away again.

+ + +

When I open my eyes, I am standing on the roof of an impossibly high building, right near the ledge. Beneath me is the hard pavement, the streets all empty, no one around to help me down. Wind buffets me from all angles, and I tilt back, falling on my back on the gravel roof.

I don't even like being up here, seeing the wide, empty sky around me, reminding me that I am at the tallest point in the city. I remember that Jeanine Matthews is watching; I throw myself against the door to the roof, trying to pull it open as I form a strategy. My usual way to face this fear would be to leap off the ledge of the building, knowing that it's just a simulation and I won't actually die. But someone else in this simulation would never do that; they would find a safe way to get down.

I evaluate my options. I can try to get this door open, but there are no tools that will help me do that around here, just the gravel roof and the door and the sky. I can't create a tool to get through the door, because that's exactly the kind of simulation manipulation that Jeanine is probably looking for. I back up, kicking the door hard with my heel, and it doesn't budge.

My heart pounding in my throat, I walk to the ledge again. Instead of looking all the way down at the minuscule sidewalks beneath me, I look at the building itself. There are windows with ledges beneath me, hundreds of them. The fastest way down, the most Dauntless way, is to scale the side of the building.

I put my face in my hands. I know this isn't real, but it feels real, the wind whistling in my ears, crisp and cool, the concrete rough beneath my hands, the sound of the gravel scattered by my shoes. I put one leg over the ledge, shuddering, and turn to face the building as I lower myself down, one leg at a time, until I'm hanging by my fingertips from the ledge.

Panic bubbles up inside me, and I scream into my teeth. *Oh God.* I hate heights—I *hate* them. I blink tears from my eyes, internally blaming them on the wind, and feel with my toes for the window ledge beneath me. Finding it, I feel for the top of the window with one hand, and press up to keep my balance as I lower myself onto the balls of my feet on the windowsill below me.

My body tilts back, over the empty space, and I scream again, clenching my teeth so hard they squeak.

I have to do that again. And again. And again.

I bend, holding the top of the window with one hand and the bottom with the other. When I have a good grip, I slide my toes down the side of the building, listening to them scrape on the stone, and let myself dangle again.

This time, when I let myself drop onto the other ledge, I don't hold on hard enough with my hands. I lose my footing on the windowsill and tip back. I scramble, scratching at the concrete building with my fingertips, but it's too late; I plummet, and another scream rises up inside me, tearing from my throat. I could create a net beneath me; I could create a rope in the air to save me—no, I shouldn't create anything or they will know what I can do.

I let myself fall. I let myself die.

I wake with pain—created by my mind—singing in every part of my body, screaming, my eyes blurry with tears and terror. I jerk forward, gasping. My body is shaking; I'm ashamed to be acting this way with this audience, but I know that it's a good thing. It will show them that I'm not special—I'm just another reckless Dauntless who thought he could scale a building and failed.

"Interesting," Jeanine says, and I can barely hear her over my own breathing. "I never tire of seeing inside a person's mind—every detail suggests so much."

I put my legs—still shaking—over the edge of the chair and plant my feet on the ground.

"You did well," Amar says. "Your climbing skills are maybe a little wanting, but you still got out of the simulation quickly, like last time."

He smiles at me. I must have succeeded at pretending to be normal, because he doesn't look worried anymore.

I nod.

"Well, it appears that your abnormal test result was a program error. We will have to investigate the simulation program to find the flaw," Jeanine says. "Now, Amar. I'd like to see one of *your* fear simulations, if you wouldn't mind obliging."

"Mine? Why mine?"

Jeanine's mild smile doesn't change. "Our information suggests that you were not alarmed by Tobias's abnormal result—that you were quite familiar with it, in fact. So I would like to see if that familiarity comes from experience."

"Your information," Amar says. "Information from where?"

"An initiate came forward to express his concerns for your and Tobias's well-being," Jeanine says. "I would like to respect his privacy. Tobias, you may leave now. Thank you for your assistance."

I look at Amar. He nods a little. I push myself to my feet, still a little unsteady, and walk out, leaving the door cracked open so I can stay and eavesdrop. But as soon as I'm in the hallway, Jeanine's assistant pushes the door shut, and I can't hear anything behind it, even when I press my ear to it.

An initiate came forward to express his concerns—and I'm sure I know who that initiate is. Our only former Erudite: Eric.

+ + +

For a week, it seems that nothing will come of Jeanine Matthews's visit. All the initiates, Dauntless-born and transfer alike, go through fear simulations every day, and every day, I allow myself to be consumed by my own fears: heights, confinement, violence, Marcus. Sometimes they blur together, Marcus at the top of tall buildings, violence in confined spaces. I always wake half-delirious, shaking, embarrassed that even though I am the initiate with only four fears, I am also the one who can't dispel them when the simulations are done. They creep up on me when I least expect them, filling my sleep with nightmares and my waking with shudders and paranoia. I grind my teeth, I jump at small noises, my hands go numb without warning. I worry that I will go insane before initiation is done.

"You okay?" Zeke asks me at breakfast one morning. "You look . . . exhausted."

"I'm fine," I say, harsher than I mean to be.

"Oh, clearly," Zeke says, grinning. "It's okay to not be okay, you know."

"Yeah, right," I say, and I force myself to finish my food, even though it all tastes like dust to me, these days. If I have to feel like I'm losing my mind, I'm at least putting on weight—muscle, mostly. It's strange to take up so much space just by existing when I used to disappear so easily.

It makes me feel just a little stronger, a little more stable.

Zeke and I put our trays away. When we're on our way out to the Pit, Zeke's little brother—Uriah is his name, I remember—runs up to us. He's taller than Zeke already, with a bandage behind his ear that covers up a fresh tattoo. Usually he looks like he's constantly on the verge of making a joke, but not right now. Right now he just looks stunned.

"Amar," he says, a little breathless. "Amar is . . ." He shakes his head. "Amar is dead."

I laugh a little. Distantly I'm aware that that's not an appropriate reaction, but I can't help it. "What? What do you mean, he's *dead*?"

"A Dauntless woman found a body on the ground near the Pire early this morning," Uriah says. "They just identified it. It was Amar. He . . . he must have . . ."

"Jumped?" Zeke says.

"Or fell, no one knows," Uriah says.

I move toward the paths climbing the walls of the Pit. Usually I almost press my body to the wall when I do this, afraid of the height, but this time I don't even think about what's below me. I brush past running, shrieking children and the people going into shops, coming out of them. I climb the staircase that dangles from the glass ceiling.

A crowd is gathered in the lobby of the Pire. I elbow my way through it. Some people curse at me, or elbow me back, but I don't really notice. I make my way to the edge of the room, to the glass walls above the streets that surround the Dauntless compound. Out there, there's an area sectioned off with tape, and a streak of dark red on the pavement.

I stare at the streak for a long time, until I feel myself comprehending that that streak comes from Amar's blood, from his body colliding with the ground.

Then I walk away.

+++

I didn't know Amar well enough to feel grief, in the way I've taught myself to think of it. Grief was what I felt after my mother's death, a weight that made it impossible to move through each day. I remember stopping in the middle of simple tasks to rest, and forgetting to start them again, or waking up in the middle of the night with tears on my face.

I don't carry Amar's loss like that. I find myself feeling it every now and then, when I remember how he gave me my name, how he protected me when he didn't even know me. But most of the time I just feel angry. His death had something to do with Jeanine Matthews and the evaluation of his fear simulation, I know it. And that means that whatever happened is also Eric's responsibility, because he overheard our conversation and told his former faction leader about it.

They killed Amar, the Erudite. But everyone thinks that he jumped, or fell. It's something a Dauntless would do.

The Dauntless have a memorial service for him that evening. Everyone is drunk by late afternoon. We gather by the chasm, and Zeke passes me a cup of dark liquid, and I swallow it all without thinking. As the liquid calm moves through me, I sway a little on my feet and pass the empty cup back to him.

"Yeah, that seems about right," Zeke says, staring into the empty cup. "I'm going to get some more."

I nod and listen to the roar of the chasm. Jeanine Matthews seemed to accept that my own abnormal results were just a problem with the program, but what if that was just an act? What if she comes after me the way she came after Amar? I try to push the thought down where I won't find it again.

A dark, scarred hand falls on my shoulder, and Max stands beside me.

"You all right, Four?" he says.

"Yeah," I say, and it's true, I am all right. I am all right because I'm still on my feet and I'm not yet slurring my words.

"I know Amar took a particular interest in you. I think

he saw strong potential." Max smiles a little.

"I didn't really know him," I say.

"He was always a little troubled, a little unbalanced. Not like the rest of the initiates in his class," Max says. "I think losing his grandparents really took a toll on him. Or maybe the problem was deeper. . . . I don't know. It could be that he's better off this way."

"Better off *dead*?" I say, scowling at him.

"That's not exactly what I meant," Max says. "But here in Dauntless, we encourage our members to choose their own paths through life. If this is what he chose . . . so much the better." He puts his hand on my shoulder again. "Depending on how you do in your final examination tomorrow, you and I should talk about the future you'd like to have here in Dauntless. You're by far our most promising initiate, despite your background."

I just keep staring at him. I don't even understand what he's saying, or why he's saying it here, at Amar's memorial service. Is he trying to *recruit* me? For what?

Zeke returns with two cups, and Max melts into the crowd like nothing ever happened. One of Amar's friends stands on a chair and shouts something meaningless about Amar being brave enough to explore the unknown.

Everyone lifts their glasses and chants his name. *Amar, Amar, Amar.* They say it so many times that it loses all meaning, the noise relentless and repetitive and all-consuming.

Then we all drink. This is how the Dauntless mourn: by chasing grief into the oblivion of alcohol and leaving it there.

All right. Fine. I can chase it too.

+++

My final examination, my fear landscape, is administered by Tori and observed by the Dauntless leaders, including Max. I go somewhere in the middle of the pack of the initiates, and for the first time, I'm not even a little bit nervous. In the fear landscape, everyone is aware during the simulation, so I have nothing to hide. I jab myself in the neck with the needle and let reality disappear.

I've done it dozens of times. I find myself at the top of a high building and run off the edge. I get shut into a box and allow myself a brief moment of panic before slamming my shoulder into the right wall, shattering the wood with the impact, impossibly. I pick up a gun and shoot an innocent person—this time a faceless man dressed in Dauntless black—in the head without even thinking about it.

This time, when the Marcuses surround me, they look more like him than they did before. His mouth is a mouth, though his eyes are still empty pits. And when he draws back his arm to hit me, he's holding a belt, not a barbed chain or some other weapon that can tear me apart piece by piece. I take a few hits, then dive at the nearest Marcus, wrapping my hands around his throat. I punch wildly at his face, and the violence gives me just a brief moment of satisfaction before I wake up, crouched on the floor of the fear landscape room.

The lights go on in the room beyond this one, so I can see the people inside it. There are two rows of waiting initiates, including Eric, who now has so many piercings in his lip that I find myself daydreaming about yanking them out one by one. Sitting in front of them are the three Dauntless leaders, including Max, all of whom are nodding and smiling. Tori gives me a thumbs-up.

I went into the examination thinking I didn't care anymore, not about passing, not about doing well, not about being Dauntless. But Tori's thumbs-up makes me swell with pride, and I let myself smile a little when I walk out. Amar may be dead, but he always wanted me to do well. I can't say I did it for him—I didn't really do it for anyone, not even myself. But at least I didn't embarrass him.

All the initiates who are finished with their final examination wait for the results in the transfer dormitory, Dauntless-borns and transfers alike. Zeke and

Shauna whoop when I come in, and I sit down on the edge of my bed.

"How'd it go?" Zeke asks me.

"Fine," I say. "No surprises. Yours?"

"Awful, but I made it out alive," he says, shrugging. "Shauna got some new ones, though."

"I handled them," Shauna says with exaggerated nonchalance. She has a pillow across her knees, one of Eric's. He won't like that.

Her act breaks, and she grins. "I was pretty awesome."

"Yeah, yeah," Zeke says.

Shauna smacks him with the pillow, right in the face. He snatches it from her.

"What do you want me to say? Yes, you were awesome. Yes, you're the best Dauntless ever. Happy?" He hits her in the shoulder with the pillow. "She's been bragging nonstop since we started the fear sims because she's better at them than I am. It's annoying."

"It's just revenge for how much you bragged during combat training," she says. "'Did you see that great hit I got right in the beginning?' Blah, blah, blah."

She pushes him, and he grabs her wrists. She breaks free and flicks his ear, and they're laughing, fighting.

I may not understand Dauntless affection, but

apparently I know flirtation when I see it. I smirk. I guess that resolves the Shauna question, not that it was really plaguing me. That was probably an answer in and of itself.

We sit around for another hour as the others finish their final exams, trickling in one after another. The last one to come in is Eric, and he just stands in the doorway, looking smug.

"Time to get our results," he says.

The others all get up and walk past him on their way out. Some of them seem nervous; others look cocky, sure of themselves. I wait until they're all gone before I walk to the doorway, but I don't go through it. I stop, crossing my arms and staring at Eric for a few seconds.

"Got something to say?" he says.

"I know it was you," I say. "Who told the Erudite about Amar. I know."

"I don't know what you're talking about," he says, but it's obvious that he does.

"You're the reason he's dead," I say. I'm surprised by how quickly the anger comes on. My body quakes with it, my face hot.

"Did you get hit in the head during your exam, Stiff?" Eric says, smirking. "You're not making any sense."

I shove him back, hard, against the door. Then I hold

him there with one arm—I'm surprised, for a moment, how much stronger I am—and lean in close to his face. "I know it was you," I say, searching his black eyes for something, anything. I see nothing, just dead-fish eyes, impenetrable. "You're the reason he's dead, and you won't get away with it."

I let him go and walk down the hallway toward the cafeteria.

+ + +

The dining hall is *packed* with people dressed in their Dauntless best—all piercings exaggerated by flashier rings, all tattoos on display, even if it means going without clothing. I try to keep my eyes on people's faces as I navigate through the crush of bodies. The scents of cake and cooked meat and bread and spices are on the air, making my mouth water—I forgot to eat lunch.

When I reach my usual table, I steal a roll from Zeke's plate when he's not looking and stand with the others to wait for our results. I hope they won't make us wait too long. I feel like I'm holding a live wire, my hands twitching and my thoughts frantic, scattered. Zeke and Shauna try to talk to me, but none of us can shout loud enough over the noise for them to hear me, so we resign ourselves to waiting without speaking.

Max gets on one of the tables and holds up his hands for quiet. He mostly gets it, though even he can't completely silence the Dauntless, some of whom go on talking and joking like nothing ever happened. Still, I can hear him as he gives his speech.

"A few weeks ago, a group of scrawny, scared initiates gave their blood to the coals and made the big jump into Dauntless," Max says. "To be honest, I didn't think any of them would make it through the first day"—he pauses to allow for laughter, and it comes, even though it wasn't a very good joke—"but I'm pleased to announce that this year, all of our initiates attained the required scores necessary to become Dauntless!"

Everyone cheers. Despite the assurance that they won't be cut, Zeke and Shauna exchange nervous looks—the order in which we are ranked still determines what kind of job we can choose in Dauntless. Zeke puts his arm across Shauna's shoulders and squeezes.

I feel suddenly alone again.

"No more delays," Max says. "I know our initiates are jumping out of their skin. So, here are our twelve new Dauntless members!"

The initiates' names appear on a large screen behind him, large enough even for people at the back of the room to see. I search the list automatically for their names:

6. *Zeke*

7. *Ash*

8. *Shauna*

Instantly, some of my tension disappears. I follow the list up, and panic stabs me for just a second when I can't find my own name. But then, there it is, right at the top.

1. *Four*

2. *Eric*

Shauna lets out a yell, and she and Zeke crush me into a sloppy hug, their weight almost knocking me to the ground. I laugh and bring my arms up to return the gesture.

Somewhere in the chaos, I dropped my dinner roll—I crush it under my heel and smile as people surround me, people I don't even know, slapping my shoulders and grinning and saying my name. My name, which is only "Four" now, all suspicions about my origin and my identity forgotten now that I am one of them, now that I am Dauntless.

I am not Tobias Eaton, not anymore, never again. I am Dauntless.

+++

That night, dizzy with excitement and so full of food I can hardly walk, I slip away from the celebration and climb the paths to the top of the Pit, to the lobby of the Pire. I walk out of the doors and suck in a deep breath of the night air, which is cool and refreshing, unlike the hot, close air in the cafeteria.

I walk toward the train tracks, too full of manic energy to stay still. There is a train coming, the light fixed to its front car blinking as it comes toward me. It charges past with power and energy, loud as thunder in my ears. I lean closer to it, for the first time savoring the thrill of fear in my stomach, to be so close to such a dangerous thing.

Then I see something dark and human-like standing in one of the last cars. A tall, lean female figure, leaning out of the car, holding on to one of the handles. For just a second as the blur of the train passes me, I see dark, curly hair and a hooked nose.

She looks almost like my mother.

And then she's gone, gone with the train.

THE SON

THE SMALL APARTMENT is bare, the floor still streaked with broom strokes at the corners. I don't own anything to fill the space except my Abnegation clothes, which are stuffed into the bottom of the bag at my side. I throw it on the bare mattress and check the drawers beneath the bed for sheets.

The Dauntless lottery was kind to me, because I was ranked first, and because unlike my outgoing fellow initiates, I wanted to live alone. The others, like Zeke and Shauna, grew up surrounded by Dauntless community, and to them the silence and the stillness of living alone would be unbearable.

I make the bed quickly, pulling the top sheet taut, so it almost has corners. The sheets are worn in places, from moths or from prior use, I'm not sure. The blanket, a blue quilt, smells like cedar and dust. When I open the bag that contains my meager possessions, I hold the Abnegation shirt—torn, from where I had to tear away fabric to bind the wound in my hand—in front of me. It looks small—I doubt I could even fit into it if I tried to put it on now, but I don't try, I just fold it and drop it in the drawer.

I hear a knock, and I say, "Come in!" thinking it's Zeke or Shauna. But Max, a tall man with dark skin and bruised knuckles, walks into my apartment, his hands folded in front of him. He surveys the room once and curls his lip with disgust at the gray slacks folded on my bed. The reaction surprises me a little—there aren't many in this city who would choose Abnegation as their faction, but there aren't many who hate it, either. Apparently I've found one of them.

I stand, unsure what to say. There's a faction leader in my apartment.

"Hello," I say.

"Sorry to interrupt," he says. "I'm surprised you didn't choose to room with your fellow former initiates. You did make some friends, didn't you?"

"Yeah," I say. "This just feels more normal."

"I guess it'll take you some time to let go of your old faction." Max skims the counter in my small kitchen with a fingertip, looks at the dust he collected, then wipes his hand on his pants. He gives me a critical look—one that tells me to let go of my old faction faster. If I was still an initiate, I might worry about that look, but I'm a Dauntless member now, and he can't take that away from me, no matter how "Stiff" I seem.

Can he?

"This afternoon you'll pick your job," Max says. "Did you have anything in mind?"

"I guess it depends on what's available," I say. "I'd like to do something with teaching. Like what Amar did, maybe."

"I think the first-ranked initiate can do a little better than 'initiation instructor,' don't you?" Max's eyebrows lift, and I notice that one doesn't move as much as the other—it's crossed with a scar. "I came because an opportunity has opened up."

He pulls a chair out from under the small table near the kitchen counter, turns it, and sits on it backward. His black boots are caked with light-brown mud and the laces are knotted and fraying at the ends. He might be the oldest Dauntless I've ever seen, but he may as well be made of steel.

"To be honest, one of my fellow leaders of Dauntless is getting a little old for the job," Max says. I sit on the edge of the bed. "The remaining four of us think it would be a good idea to get some new blood in leadership. New ideas for new Dauntless members and initiation, specifically. That task is usually given to the youngest leader anyway, so it's a good fit. We were thinking of drawing from the more recent initiate classes for a training program to see if anyone is a good candidate. You're a natural choice."

I feel like my skin is too tight for me, suddenly. Is he really suggesting that at the age of sixteen I could qualify as a Dauntless leader?

"The training program will last at least a year," Max says. "It will be rigorous and it will test your skills in a lot of areas. We both know you'll do just fine in the fear landscape portion."

I nod without thinking. He must not mind my self-assuredness, because he smiles a little.

"You won't need to go to the job selection meeting later today," Max says. "Training will start very soon—tomorrow morning, in fact."

"Wait," I say, a thought breaking through the muddle in my mind. "I don't have a choice?"

"Of course you have a choice." He looks puzzled. "I just assumed someone like you would rather train to be a leader than spend all day standing around a fence with a gun on his shoulder, or lecturing initiates about good fighting technique. But if I was wrong . . ."

I don't know why I'm hesitating. I don't want to spend my days guarding the fence, or patrolling the city, or even pacing the training room floor. I may have an aptitude for fighting, but that doesn't mean I want to do it all day, every day. The chance to make a difference in Dauntless appeals to the Abnegation parts of me, the parts that are lingering around, occasionally demanding attention.

I think I just don't like when I'm not given a choice.

I shake my head. "No, you weren't wrong." I clear my throat and try to sound stronger, more determined. "I want to do it. Thank you."

"Excellent." Max gets up and cracks one of his knuckles idly, like it's an old habit. He holds out his hand for me to shake, and I take it, though the gesture is still unfamiliar to me—the Abnegation would never touch each other so casually. "Come to the conference room near my office tomorrow morning at eight. It's in the Pire. Tenth floor."

He leaves, scattering bits of dried earth from the bottom of his shoes as he walks out. I sweep them up with the broom that leans against the wall near the door. It's not until I'm scooting the chair back under the table that I realize—if I become a Dauntless leader, a representative of my faction, I'll have to come face-to-face with my father again. And not just once but constantly, until he finally retires into Abnegation obscurity.

My fingers start to go numb. I've faced my fears so many times in simulations, but that doesn't mean I'm ready to face them in reality.

+ + +

"Dude, you missed it!" Zeke is wide-eyed, concerned. "The only jobs left by the end were the gross jobs, like scrubbing toilets! Where *were* you?"

"It's fine," I say as I carry my tray back to our table near the doors. Shauna is there with her little sister, Lynn, and Lynn's friend Marlene. When I first saw them there, I wanted to turn around and leave immediately—Marlene is too cheerful for me even on a good day—but Zeke had already seen me, so it was too late. Behind us, Uriah jogs to catch up, his plate loaded with more food than he can possibly pack into his stomach. "I didn't miss anything— Max came to see me earlier."

As we take our seats at the table, under one of the bright-blue lamps that hang from the wall, I tell him about Max's offer, careful not to make it sound too impressive. I only just found friends; I don't want to create jealous tension between us for no reason. When I finish, Shauna leans her face into one of her hands and says to Zeke, "I guess we should have tried harder during initiation, huh?"

"Or killed him before he could take his final test."

"Or both." Shauna grins at me. "Congrats, Four. You deserve it."

I feel everyone's eyes on me like distinct, powerful beams of heat, and hurry to change the subject. "Where did you guys end up?"

"Control room," Zeke says. "My mom used to work there, and she taught me most of what I'll need to know already."

"I'm in the patrol leadership track . . . thing," Shauna says. "Not the most exciting job ever, but at least I'll get to be outside."

"Yeah, let's hear you say that in the dead of winter when you're trudging through a foot of snow and ice," Lynn says sourly. She stabs at a pile of mashed potatoes with her fork. "I better do well in initiation. I don't want to get stuck at the fence."

"Didn't we talk about this?" Uriah says. "Don't say the 'I' word until at most two weeks before it happens. It makes me want to throw up."

I look at the pile of food on his tray. "Stuffing yourself up to your eyeballs with food, though, that's fine?"

He rolls his eyes at me and bends over his tray to keep eating. I poke at my own food—I haven't had any appetite since this morning, too worried about tomorrow to stand a full stomach.

Zeke spots someone across the cafeteria. "I'll be right back."

Shauna watches him cross the room to greet a few young Dauntless members. They don't look much older than he is, but I don't recognize them from initiation, so they must be a year or two older. Zeke says something to the group—mostly made up of girls—that sends them into fits of laughter, and he jabs one of the girls in the ribs, making her squeal. Beside me, Shauna glowers and misses her mouth with her fork, smearing sauce from the chicken all over her cheek. Lynn snorts into her food, and Marlene kicks her—audibly—under the table.

"So," Marlene says loudly. "Do you know of anyone else who's doing that leadership program, Four?"

"Come to think of it, I didn't see Eric there today, either," Shauna says. "I was hoping he tripped and fell into the chasm, but . . ."

I shove a bite of food in my mouth and try not to think about it. The blue light makes my hands look blue, too, like the hands of a corpse. I haven't spoken to Eric since I accused him of being indirectly responsible for Amar's death—someone reported Amar's simulation aware-ness to Jeanine Matthews, leader of Erudite, and as a former Erudite, Eric is the most likely suspect. I haven't decided what I'll do the next time I have to talk to him, either. Beating him up again isn't going to prove that he's a faction traitor. I'll have to find some way to connect his recent activities to the Erudite and take the information to one of the Dauntless leaders—Max, probably, since I know him best.

Zeke walks back to the table and slides into his seat. "Four. What are you doing tomorrow night?"

"I don't know," I say. "Nothing?"

"Not anymore," he says. "You're coming with me on a date."

I choke on my next bite of potatoes. "What?"

"Um, hate to tell you this, big brother," Uriah says, "but you're supposed to go on dates alone, not bring a friend."

"It's a double date, obviously," Zeke says. "I asked Maria out, and she said something about finding a date for her friend Nicole, and I indicated that you would be interested."

"Which one's Nicole?" Lynn says, craning her neck to look at the group of girls.

"The redhead," Zeke says. "So, eight o'clock. You're in, I'm not even asking."

"I don't—" I say. I look at the redheaded girl across the room. She's fair-skinned, with wide eyes smeared with black, and wearing a tight shirt, which shows off the bend in her waist and . . . other things my inner Abnegation voice tells me not to notice. I do anyway.

I've never been on a date, thanks to my former faction's strict courtship rituals, involving engaging in acts of service together and maybe—*maybe*—having dinner with someone else's family and helping them clean up afterward. I've never even thought about whether I wanted to date anyone; it was such an impossibility. "Zeke, I've never—"

Uriah frowns and pokes my arm, hard, with one finger. I slap his hand away. *"What?"*

"Oh, nothing," Uriah says cheerfully. "You were just sounding *Stiffer* than usual, so I thought I would check—"

Marlene laughs. "Yeah, right."

Zeke and I exchange a look. We've never explicitly talked about not sharing my faction of origin, but as far as I know, he's never mentioned it to anyone. Uriah knows, but despite his loud mouth, he seems to understand when to withhold information. Still, I'm not sure why Marlene hasn't figured it out—maybe she's not very observant.

"It's not a big deal, Four," Zeke says. He eats his last bite of food. "You'll go, you'll talk to her like she's a normal human being—which she *is*—maybe she'll let you—*gasp*—*hold her hand*—"

Shauna gets up suddenly, her chair screeching on the stone floor. She tucks her hair behind one ear and walks toward the tray return, head down. Lynn glares at Zeke—which hardly looks different from her normal facial expression—and follows her sister across the cafeteria.

"Okay, you don't have to hold hands with anyone," Zeke says, like nothing happened. "Just go, all right? I'll owe you one."

I look at Nicole. She's sitting at a table near the tray return and laughing at someone else's joke again. Maybe Zeke's right—maybe it's not that big a deal, and maybe this is another way that I can unlearn my Abnegation past and learn to embrace my Dauntless future. And besides—she's pretty.

"Okay," I say. "I'll go. But if you make some kind of joke about hand holding, I'm going to break your nose."

+ + +

When I get back to my apartment that night, it still smells like dust and a hint of mold. I turn on one of the lamps, and a glimmer of light reflects off the countertop. I run my hand over it, and a small piece of glass pricks my finger, making it bleed. I pinch it between my fingertips and carry it to the trash can, which I put a bag in this morning. But resting at the bottom of the bag now is a pile of shards in the shape of a drinking glass.

I haven't used one of those yet.

A shiver goes down my spine, and I scan the rest of the apartment for signs of disruption. The sheets aren't rumpled, none of the drawers are open, none of the chairs seem to have moved. But I would know if I had broken a glass that morning.

So who was in my apartment?

+++

I don't know why, but the first thing my hands find in the morning when I stumble into the bathroom is the set of hair clippers I got with my Dauntless credits yesterday. And then while I'm still blinking the clouds from my eyes, I turn them on and touch them to my head the way I've done since I was young. I bend my ear forward to protect it from the blades; I know just how to twist and shift so that I can see as much of the back of my head as possible. The ritual calms my nerves, makes me feel focused and steady. I brush the trimmed hairs from my shoulders and neck and sweep them into the wastebasket.

It's an Abnegation morning. A quick shower, a plain breakfast, a clean house. Except I'm wearing Dauntless black, boots and pants and shirt and jacket. I avoid looking in the mirror on my way out, and it makes me grit my teeth, knowing how deep these Stiff roots go, and how hard it will be to excise them from my mind, as tangled up in everything as they are. I left that place out of fear and defiance, and that will make it harder to assimilate than anyone knows, harder than if I had actually chosen Dauntless for the right reasons.

I walk quickly toward the Pit, emerging through an arch halfway up the wall. I stay away from the edge of the path, though Dauntless children, shrieking with laughter, sometimes run right along it, and I should be braver than they are. I'm not sure bravery is something you acquire more of with age, like wisdom—but maybe here, in Dauntless, bravery is the highest form of wisdom, the acknowledgment that life can and should be lived without fear.

It's the first time I've found myself being thoughtful about Dauntless life, so I hold on to the thought as I ascend the paths around the Pit. I reach the staircase that hangs from the glass ceiling and keep my eyes up, away from the space opening up beneath me, so I don't start to panic. But my heart is pounding by the time I reach the top anyway; I can feel it even in my throat. Max said his office was on the tenth floor, so I ride the elevator up with a group of Dauntless going to work. They don't all seem to know one another, unlike the Abnegation—it's not as important to them to memorize names and faces and needs and wants, so maybe they just keep to their friends and families, forming rich but separate communities within their faction. Like the one I'm forming myself.

When I reach the tenth floor, I'm not sure where to go, but then I spot a dark head turning a corner in front of me. Eric. I follow him, partly because he probably knows where he's going, but partly because I want to know what he's doing even if he's not going to the same place I am. But when I turn the corner, I see Max standing in a conference room that has glass walls, surrounded by young Dauntless. The oldest one is maybe twenty, and the youngest is probably not much older than I am. Max sees me through the glass and motions for me to come in. Eric sits close to him—*Suck-up*, I think—but I sit at the other end of the table, between a girl with a ring through her nostrils and a boy whose hair is such a bright shade of green I can't look straight at him. I feel plain by comparison—I may have gotten Dauntless flames tattooed on my side during initiation, but it's not like they're on display.

"I think everyone is here, so let's get started." Max closes the door to the conference room and stands before us. He looks strange in such an ordinary environment, like he's here to break all the glass and cause chaos rather than lead this meeting. "You're all here because you've shown potential, first, but also because you've displayed enthusiasm for our faction and its future." I don't know how I've done that. "Our city is changing, faster now than ever before, and in order to keep up with it, we'll have to change, too. We'll have to become stronger, braver, better than we are now. And among you are the people who can get us there, but we'll have to figure out who they are. We'll be doing a combination of instruction and skills tests for the next several months, to teach you what you'll need to know if you make it through this program, but also to see how quickly you learn." That sounds a little like something the Erudite would value, not the Dauntless—strange.

"The first thing you'll do is fill out this info sheet," he says, and I almost laugh. There's something ridiculous about a tough, hardened Dauntless warrior with a stack of papers he calls "info sheets," but of course some things have to be ordinary, because it's more efficient that way. He sends the stack around the table, along with a bundle of pens. "All this will do is tell us more about you and give us a starting point by which to measure your progress. So it's in your best interest to be honest, and not to make yourself sound better than you are."

I feel unsettled, staring at the sheet of paper. I fill out my name—which is the first question—and my age—the second. The third asks for my faction of origin, and the fourth asks for my number of fears. The fifth asks what those fears are.

I'm not sure how to describe them. The first two are easy—heights, confinement—but the next one? And what am I supposed to write about my father, that I'm afraid of Marcus Eaton? Eventually I scribble *losing control* for my third fear and *physical threats in confined spaces* for my fourth, knowing that that's far from true.

But the next few questions are strange, confusing. They're statements, trickily worded, that I'm supposed to agree or disagree with. *It's okay to steal if it's to help someone else.* Well, that's easy enough—agree. *Some people are more deserving of rewards than others.* Maybe. It depends on the rewards. *Power should be given only to those who earn it. Difficult circumstances form stronger people. You don't know how strong a person really is until they're tested.* I glance around the table at the others. Some people seem puzzled, but no one looks the way I feel—disturbed, almost afraid to circle an answer beneath each statement.

I don't know what to do, so I circle "agree" for each one and pass my sheet back with everyone else's.

+++

Zeke and his date, Maria, are pressed up against a wall in a hallway next to the Pit. I can see their silhouettes from here. It looks like they're still just as pressed-up-against-each-other as they were five minutes ago when they first went back there, giggling like idiots the whole time. I cross my arms and look back at Nicole.

"So," I say.

"So," she says, tipping forward onto the balls of her feet and back onto her heels again. "This is a little awkward, right?"

"Yeah," I say, relieved. "It is."

"How long have you been friends with Zeke?" she says. "I haven't seen you around much."

"A few weeks," I say. "We met during initiation."

"Oh," she says. "Were you a transfer?"

"Um . . ." I don't want to admit that I transferred from Abnegation, partly because whenever I admit that, people start thinking I'm uptight, and partly because I don't like to toss out hints about my parentage when I can avoid it. I decide to lie. "No, just . . . kept to myself before then, I guess."

"Oh." She narrows her eyes a little. "You must have been really good at it."

"One of my specialties," I say. "How long have you been friends with Maria?"

"Since we were kids. She could trip and fall and land on a date with someone," Nicole says. "Others of us aren't as talented."

"Yeah." I shake my head. "Zeke had to push me into this a little."

"Really." Nicole raises an eyebrow. "Did he at least show you what you were in for?"

She points at herself.

"Um, yeah," I say. "I wasn't sure if you were my type, but I thought maybe—"

"Not your type." She sounds cold, suddenly. I try to backtrack.

"I mean, I don't think that's that important," I say. "Personality is much more important than—"

"Than my unsatisfactory looks?" She raises both eyebrows.

"That's not what I said," I say. "I'm . . . really terrible at this."

"Yeah," she says. "You are."

She grabs the small black bag that was resting against her feet and tucks it under her arm. "Tell Maria I had to go home early."

She stalks away from the railing and disappears into one of the paths next to the Pit. I sigh and look at Zeke and Maria again. I can tell by the faint movements I'm able to detect that they haven't slowed down at all. I tap my fingers against the railing. Now that our double date has become an awkward, triangle-shaped date, it must be all right for me to leave.

I spot Shauna coming out of the cafeteria and wave to her.

"Isn't tonight your big date night with Ezekiel?" she says.

"*Ezekiel*," I say, cringing. "I forgot that was his whole name. Yeah, my date just stormed off."

"Good one," she says, laughing. "What'd you last, ten minutes?"

"Five," I say, and I find myself laughing, too. "Apparently I'm insensitive."

"No," she says with mock surprise. "You? But you're so sentimental and sweet!"

"Funny," I say. "Where's Lynn?"

"She started arguing with Hector. Our little brother," she says. "And I've been listening to them do that for, oh, my whole life. So I left. I thought I'd go to the training room, get some exercise in. Want to go?"

"Yeah," I say. "Let's go."

We head toward the training room, but then I realize that we have to walk down the same hallway that Zeke and Maria currently occupy to get there. I try to stop Shauna with a hand, but I'm too late—she sees their two bodies pressed together, her eyes wide. She pauses for a moment, and I hear smacking noises I wish I hadn't heard. Then she moves down the hallway again, walking so fast I have to jog to catch up to her.

"Shauna—"

"Training room," she says.

When we get there, she starts immediately on the punching bag, and I've never seen her hit so hard before.

+ + +

"Though it might seem strange, it's important for high-level Dauntless to understand how a few programs work," Max says. "The surveillance program in the control room is an obvious one—a Dauntless leader will sometimes have to monitor the things happening in the faction. Then there's the simulation programs, which you have to understand in order to evaluate Dauntless initiates. Also the currency tracking program, which keeps commerce in our faction running smoothly, among others. Some of these programs are pretty sophisticated, which means you'll have to be able to learn computer skills easily, if you don't already have them. That's what we'll be doing today."

He gestures to the woman standing at his left shoulder. I recognize her from the game of Dare. She's young, with purple streaks in her short hair and more piercings than I can easily count.

"Lauren here will be teaching you some of the basics, and

then we'll test you," Max says. "Lauren is one of our initiation instructors, but in her downtime she works as a computer technician in Dauntless headquarters. It's a little Erudite of her, but we'll let it slide for the sake of convenience."

Max winks at her, and she grins.

"Go ahead," he says. "I'll be back in an hour."

Max leaves, and Lauren claps her hands together.

"Right," she says. "Today we're going to talk about how programming works. Those of you who already have some experience with this, please feel free to tune out. The rest of you better keep focused because I'm not going to repeat myself. Learning this stuff is like learning a language— it's not enough to memorize the words; you also have to understand the rules and why they work the way they do."

When I was younger, I volunteered in the computer labs in the Upper Levels building to meet my faction-mandated volunteer hours—and to get out of the house—and I learned how to take a computer apart and put it back together. But I never learned about this. The next hour passes in a blur of technical terms I can barely keep up with. I try to jot some notes on a piece of scrap paper I found on the floor, but she's moving so fast it's hard for my hand to keep up with my ears, so I abandon the effort after a few minutes and just try to pay attention. She shows examples of what she's talking about on a screen at the front of the room, and it's hard not to be distracted by the view from the windows behind her—from this angle, the Pire displays the city's skyline, the prongs of the Hub piercing the sky, the marsh peeking from between the glimmering buildings.

I'm not the only one who seems overwhelmed—the other candidates lean over to one another to whisper frantically, asking for definitions they missed. Eric, however, sits comfortably in his chair, drawing on the back of his hand. Smirking. I recognize that smirk. Of course he already knows all this stuff. He must have learned it in Erudite, probably when he was a child, or else he wouldn't look quite so smug.

Before I can really register the passage of time, Lauren is pressing a button for the display screen to withdraw into the ceiling.

"On the desktop of your computer, you'll find a file marked 'Programming Test,'" she says. "Open it. It will take you to a timed exam. You'll go through a series of small programs and mark the errors you find that are causing them to malfunction. They might be really big things, like the order of the code, or really small things, like a misplaced word or marking. You don't have to fix them right now, but you do have to be able to spot them. There will be one error per program. Go."

Everyone starts frantically tapping at their screens.

Eric leans over to me and says, "Did your Stiff house even *have* a computer, Four?"

"No," I say.

"Well, you see, this is how you open a file," he says with an exaggerated tap on the file on his screen. "See, it looks like paper, but it's really just a picture on a screen—you know what a screen is, right?"

"Shut up," I say as I open the test.

I stare at the first program. *It's like learning a language,* I say to myself. *Everything has to start in the right order and finish in the reverse order. Just make sure that everything is in the right place.*

I don't start at the beginning of the code and make my way down—instead, I look for the innermost kernel of code inside all the wrappers. There, I notice that the line of code finishes in the wrong place. I mark the spot and press the arrow button that will allow me to continue the exam if I'm right. The screen changes, presenting me with a new program.

I raise my eyebrows. I must have absorbed more than I thought.

I start the next one in the same way, moving from the center of the code to the outside, checking the top of the program with the bottom, paying attention to quotation marks and periods and backslashes. Looking for code errors is strangely soothing, just a way of making sure that the world is still in the same order it's supposed to be, and as long as it is, everything will run smoothly.

I forget about all the people around me, even about the skyline beyond us, about what finishing this exam will mean. I just focus on what's in front of me, on the tangle of words on my screen. I notice that Eric finishes first, long before anyone else looks ready to complete their exam, but I try not to let it worry me. Even when he decides to stay next to me and look over my shoulder as I work.

Finally I touch the arrow button and a new image pops up. *EXAM COMPLETE*, it says.

"Good job," Lauren says, when she comes by to check my screen. "You're the third one to finish."

I turn toward Eric.

"Wait," I say. "Weren't you about to explain what a screen was? Obviously I have *no* computer skills at all, so I really need your help."

He glowers at me, and I grin.

+++

My apartment door is open when I return. Just an inch, but I know I closed it before I left. I nudge it open with the toe of my shoe and enter with a pounding heart, expecting to find an intruder rifling through my things, though

I'm not sure who—one of Jeanine's lackeys, searching for evidence that I'm different in the same way Amar was, maybe, or Eric, looking for a way to ambush me. But the apartment is empty and unchanged.

Unchanged—except for the piece of paper on the table. I approach it slowly, like it might burst into flames, or dissolve into the air. There's a message written on it in small, slanted handwriting.

> *On the day you hated most*
> *At the time when she died*
> *In the place where you first jumped on.*

At first the words are nonsense to me, and I think they're a joke, something left here to rattle me, and it worked, because I feel unsteady on my feet. I sit in one of the rickety chairs, hard, without moving my eyes from the paper. I read it over and over again, and the message starts to take shape in my mind.

In the place where you first jumped on. That must mean the train platform I ascended after I had just joined Dauntless.

At the time when she died. There's only one "she" this could be: my mother. My mother died in the dead of night, so that by the time I awoke, her body was already gone, whisked away by my father and his Abnegation friends. Her time of death was estimated to be around two in the morning, he said.

On the day you hated most. That's the hardest one—is it referring to a day of the year, a birthday or a holiday? None of those are coming up, and I don't see why someone would leave a note that far in advance. It must be referring to a day of the week, but what day of the week did I hate most? That's easy—council meeting days, because my father was out late and would return home in a foul mood. Wednesday.

Wednesday, two a.m., at the train platform near the Hub. That's tonight. And there's only one person in the world who would know all that information: Marcus.

+++

I'm clutching the folded piece of paper in my fist, but I can't feel it. My hands have been tingling and mostly numb since I first thought his name.

I left my apartment door wide open, and my shoes are untied. I move along the walls of the Pit without noticing how high up I am and run up the stairs to the Pire without even feeling tempted to look down. Zeke mentioned the control room's location in passing a few days ago. I can only hope he's still there now, because I'll need his help if I want to access the footage of the hallway outside my apartment. I know where the camera is, hidden in the corner where they think no one will notice it. Well, I noticed it.

My mother used to notice things like that, too. When we walked through the Abnegation sector, just the two of us, she would point out the cameras, hidden in bubbles of dark glass or fixed to the edges of buildings. She never said anything about them, or seemed worried about them, but she always knew where they were, and when she passed them, she made a point to look directly at them, as if to say, *I see you, too.* So I grew up searching, scanning, watching for details in my surroundings.

I ride the elevator to the fourth floor, then follow signs for the control room. It's down a short corridor and around the bend, the door wide open. A wall of screens greets me—a few people sit behind it, at desks, and then there are other desks along the walls where more people sit, each one with a screen of their own. The footage rotates every five seconds, showing different parts of the city—the Amity fields, the streets around the Hub, the Dauntless compound, even the Merciless Mart, with its grand lobby. I glimpse the Abnegation sector on one of the screens, then pull myself out of the daze, looking for Zeke. He's sitting at a desk on the right wall, typing something into a dialog box on the left half of his screen while footage of the Pit plays on the right half. Everyone in the room is wearing headphones—listening, I assume, to whatever they're supposed to be watching.

"Zeke," I say quietly. Some of the others look at me, as if scolding me for intruding, but no one says anything.

"Hey!" he says. "I'm glad you came, I'm bored out of my—what's wrong?"

He looks from my face to my fist, still clenched around the piece of paper. I don't know how to explain, so I don't try.

"I need to see footage from the hallway outside my apartment," I say. "From the last four or so hours. Can you help?"

"Why?" Zeke says. "What happened?"

"Someone was in my place," I say. "I want to know who it was."

He looks around, checking to make sure no one is watching. Or listening. "Listen, I can't do that—even we aren't allowed to pull up specific things unless we see something weird, it's all on a rotation—"

"You owe me a favor, remember?" I say. "I would never ask unless it was important."

"Yeah, I know." Zeke looks around again, then closes the dialog box he had open and opens another one. I watch the code he types in to call up the right footage, and I'm surprised to find that I understand some of it, after the day's lesson. An image appears on the screen, of one of the Dauntless corridors near the cafeteria. He taps it, and another image replaces it, this one of the inside of the cafeteria; the next one is of the tattoo parlor, then the hospital.

He keeps scrolling through the Dauntless compound, and I watch the images as they go past, showing momentary glimpses of ordinary Dauntless life, people playing with their piercings as they wait in line for new clothing, people practicing punches in the training room. I see a flash of Max in what appears to be his office, sitting in one of the chairs, a woman sitting across from him. A woman with blond hair tied back in a tight knot. I put my hand on Zeke's shoulder.

"Wait." The piece of paper in my fist seems a little less urgent. "Go back."

He does, and I confirm what I suspected: Jeanine Matthews is in Max's office, a folder in her lap. Her clothes are perfectly pressed, her posture straight. I take the headphones from Zeke's head, and he scowls at me but doesn't stop me.

Max's and Jeanine's voices are quiet, but I can still hear them.

"I've narrowed it down to six," Max is saying. "I'd say that's pretty good for, what? The second day?"

"This is inefficient," Jeanine says. "We already have the candidate. I ensured it. This was always the plan."

"You never asked me what I thought of the plan, and this is my faction," Max says tersely. "I don't like him, and I don't want to spend all my days working with someone I don't like. So you'll have to let me at least try to find someone else who meets all the criteria—"

"Fine." Jeanine stands, pressing her folder to her stomach. "But when you fail to do so, I expect you to admit it. I have no patience for Dauntless pride."

"Yeah, because the Erudite are the picture of humility," Max says sourly.

"Hey," Zeke hisses. "My supervisor is looking. Give me back the headphones."

He snatches them from my head, and they snap around my ears in the process, making them sting.

"You have to get out of here or I'll lose my job," Zeke says.

He looks serious, and worried. I don't object, even though I didn't find out what I needed to know—it was my own fault for getting distracted anyway. I slip out of the control room, my mind racing, half of me still terrified at the thought that my father was in my apartment, that he wants me to meet him alone on an abandoned street in the middle of the night, the other half confused by what I just heard. *We already have the candidate. I ensured it.* They must have been talking about the candidate for Dauntless leadership.

But why is Jeanine Matthews concerned with who is appointed as the next leader of Dauntless?

I make it all the way back to my apartment without noticing, then sit on the edge of the bed and stare at the opposite wall. I keep thinking separate but equally frantic thoughts. *Why does Marcus want to meet with me? Why are the Erudite so involved in Dauntless politics? Does Marcus want to kill me without witnesses, or does he want to warn me about something, or threaten me . . . ? Who was the candidate they were talking about?*

I press the heels of my hands to my forehead and try to calm down, though I feel each nervous thought like a prickle at the back of my head. I can't do anything about Max and Jeanine now. What I have to decide now is whether I'm going to this meeting tonight.

On the day you hated most. I never knew that Marcus even noticed me, noticed the things I liked or hated. He just seemed to view me as an inconvenience, an irritant. But didn't I learn a few weeks ago that he knew the simulations wouldn't work on me, and he tried to help me stay out of danger? Maybe, despite all the horrible things he's done and said to me, there's a part of him that is actually my father. Maybe that's the part of him that's inviting me to this meeting, and he's trying to show me by telling me he knows me, he knows what I hate, what I love, what I fear.

I'm not sure why that thought fills me with such hope when I've hated him for so long. But maybe, just as there's a part of him that's actually my father, there's also a part of me that's actually his son.

+++

The sun's heat is still coming off the pavement at one thirty in the morning when I leave the Dauntless compound. I can feel it on my fingertips. The moon is covered in clouds, so the streets are darker than usual, but I'm not afraid of the dark, or the streets, not anymore. That's one thing beating up a bunch of Dauntless initiates can teach you.

I breathe in the smell of warm asphalt and set off at a slow run, my sneakers slapping the ground. The streets that surround the Dauntless sector of the city are empty; my faction lives huddled together, like a pack of sleeping dogs. That's why, I realize, Max seemed so concerned about my living alone. If I'm really Dauntless, shouldn't

I want my life to overlap with theirs as much as possible, shouldn't I be looking for ways to fold myself into my faction until we are inextricable?

I consider it as I run. Maybe he's right. Maybe I'm not doing a very good job of integrating myself; maybe I'm not pushing myself hard enough. I find a steady rhythm, squinting at the street signs as I pass them, to keep track of where I'm going. I know when I reach the ring of buildings the factionless occupy because I can see their shadows moving around behind blacked-out and boarded windows. I move to run under the train tracks, the latticed wood stretching out far ahead of me and curving away from the street.

The Hub grows larger and larger in my sight as I get closer. My heart is pounding, but I don't think it's from the running. I stop abruptly when I reach the train platform, and as I stand at the foot of the stairs, catching my breath, I remember when I first climbed these steps, the sea of hooting Dauntless moving around me, pressing me forward. It was easy to be carried by their momentum then. I have to carry myself forward now. I start to climb, my footsteps echoing on the metal, and when I reach the top, I check my watch.

Two o'clock.

But the platform is empty.

I walk back and forth over it, to make sure no dark figures are hiding in dark corners. A train rumbles in the distance, and I pause to look for the light fixed to its nose. I didn't know the trains ran this late—all power in the city is supposed to shut off after midnight, to conserve energy. I wonder if Marcus asked the factionless for a special favor. But why would he travel on the train? The Marcus Eaton I know would never dare to associate himself so closely with Dauntless. He would sooner walk the streets barefoot.

The train light flashes, just once, before it careens past the platform. It pounds and churns, slowing but not stopping, and I see a person leap from the second-to-last car, lean and lithe. Not Marcus. A woman.

I squeeze the paper tighter into my fist, and tighter, until my knuckles ache.

The woman strides toward me, and when she's a few feet away, I can see her. Long curly hair. Prominent hooked nose. Black Dauntless pants, gray Abnegation shirt, brown Amity boots. Her face is lined, worn, thin. But I know her, I could never forget her face, my mother, Evelyn Eaton.

"Tobias," she breathes, wide-eyed, like she's as stunned by me as I am by her, but that's impossible. She knew I was alive, but I remember how the urn containing her ashes looked as it stood on my father's mantel, marked with his fingerprints.

I remember the day I woke to a group of grave-faced Abnegation in my father's kitchen, and how they all looked up when I entered, and how Marcus explained to me, with sympathy I knew he didn't feel, that my mother had passed in the middle of the night, complications from early labor and a miscarriage.

She was pregnant? I remember asking.

Of course she was, son. He turned to the other people in our kitchen. *Just shock, of course. Bound to happen, with something like this.*

I remember sitting with a plate full of food, in the living room, with a group of murmuring Abnegation around me, the whole neighborhood packing my house to the brim and no one saying anything that mattered to me.

"I know this must be . . . alarming for you," she says. I hardly recognize her voice; it's lower and stronger and harder than in my memories of her, and that's how I know the years have changed her. I feel too many things to manage, too powerfully to handle, and then suddenly I feel nothing at all.

"You're supposed to be dead," I say, flat. It's a stupid thing to say. Such a stupid thing to say to your mother when she comes back from the dead, but it's a stupid situation.

"I know," she says, and I think there are tears in her eyes, but it's too dark to tell. "I'm not."

"Obviously." The voice coming from my mouth is snide, casual. "Were you ever even pregnant?"

"Pregnant? Is that what they told you, something about dying in childbirth?" She shakes her head. "No, I wasn't. I had been planning my exit for months—I needed to disappear. I thought he might tell you when you were old enough."

I let out a short laugh, like a bark. "You thought that *Marcus Eaton* would admit that his wife left him. To me."

"You're his son," Evelyn says, frowning. "He loves you."

Then all the tension of the past hour, the past few weeks, the past few *years* builds inside me, too much to contain, and I really laugh, but it comes out sounding strange, mechanical. It scares me even though I'm the one doing it.

"You have a right to be angry that you were lied to," she says. "I would be angry, too. But Tobias, I had to leave, I know you understand why. . . ."

She reaches for me, and I grab her wrist, push her away. "Don't touch me."

"All right, all right." She puts her palms up and backs away. "But you do understand, you must."

"What I *understand* is that you left me alone in a house with a sadistic maniac," I say.

It looks like something inside her is collapsing. Her hands fall to her sides like two weights. Her shoulders slump. Even her face goes slack, as it dawns on her what I mean, what I must mean. I cross my arms and put my shoulders back, trying to look as big and strong and tough as possible. It's easier now, in Dauntless black, than it ever was in Abnegation gray, and maybe *that's* why I chose Dauntless as a haven. Not out of spite, not to hurt Marcus, but because I knew this life would teach me a stronger way to be.

"I—" she starts.

"Stop wasting my time. What are we doing here?" I toss the crumpled note on the ground between us and raise my eyebrows at her. "It's been seven years since you died, and you never tried to do this dramatic reveal before, so what's different now?"

At first she doesn't answer. Then she pulls herself together, visibly, and says, "We—the factionless—like to keep an eye on things. Things like the Choosing Ceremony. This time, our eye told me that you chose Dauntless. I would have gone myself, but I didn't want to risk running into *him*. I've become . . . kind of a leader to the factionless, and it's important that I don't expose myself."

I taste something sour.

"Well, well," I say. "What important parents I have. I'm so very lucky."

"This isn't like you," she says. "Is even a part of you happy to see me again?"

"Happy to see you again?" I say. "I barely remember you, Evelyn. I've almost lived as long without you as I did with you."

Her face contorts. I wounded her. I'm glad.

"When you chose Dauntless," she continues slowly, "I knew it was time to reach out to you. I've always been planning to find you, after you chose and you were on your own, so that I could invite you to join us."

"Join you," I say. "Become factionless? Why would I want to do that?"

"Our city is changing, Tobias." It's the same thing Max said yesterday. "The factionless are coming together, and so are Dauntless and Erudite. Sometime soon, everyone will have to choose a side, and I know which one you would rather be on. I think you can really make a difference with us."

"*You* know which one I'd rather be on. Really," I say. "I'm not a faction traitor. I chose Dauntless; that's where I belong."

"You aren't one of those mindless, danger-seeking fools," she snaps. "Just like you weren't a suffocated

Stiff drone. You can be more than either, more than any faction."

"You have no idea what I am or who I can be," I say. "I was the first-ranked initiate. They want me to be a Dauntless leader."

"Don't be naive," she says, narrowing her eyes at me. "They don't want a new leader; they want a pawn they can manipulate. That's why Jeanine Matthews frequents Dauntless headquarters, that's why she keeps planting minions in your faction to report on their behavior. You haven't noticed that she seems to be aware of things she has no right to be aware of, that they keep shifting Dauntless training around, experimenting with it? As if the Dauntless would ever change something like that on their own."

Amar told us the fear landscapes didn't usually come first in Dauntless initiation, that it was something new they were trying. An experiment. But she's right; the Dauntless don't do experiments. If they were really concerned with practicality and efficiency, they wouldn't bother teaching us to throw knives.

And then there's Amar, turning up dead. Wasn't I the one who accused Eric of being an informant? Haven't I suspected for weeks that he was still in touch with the Erudite?

"Even if you're right," I say, and all the malicious energy has gone out of me. I move closer to her. "Even if you're right about Dauntless, I would never join you." I try to keep my voice from wavering as I add, "I never want to see you again."

"I don't believe you," she says quietly.

"I don't care what you believe."

I move past her, toward the stairs I climbed to get up to the platform.

She calls after me, "If you change your mind, any message given to one of the factionless will go to me."

I don't look back. I run down the stairs and sprint down the street, away from the platform. I don't even know if I'm moving in the right direction, just that I want to be as far away from her as possible.

+ + +

I don't sleep.

I pace my apartment, frantic. I pull the remnants of my Abnegation life out of my drawers and dump them in the trash, the ripped shirt, the pants, the shoes, the socks, even my watch. At some point, around sunrise, I hurl the electric shaver against the shower wall, and it breaks into several pieces.

An hour after daybreak, I walk to the tattoo parlor. Tori

is already there—well, "there" might be too strong a word, because her eyes are swollen from sleep and unfocused, and she's just started on her coffee.

"Something wrong?" she said. "I'm not really here. I'm supposed to go for a run with Bud, that maniac."

"I'm hoping you'll make an exception," I say.

"Not many people come in here with urgent tattoo requests," she says.

"There's a first time for everything."

"Okay." She sits up, more alert now. "You have something in mind?"

"You had a drawing in your apartment when we walked through it a few weeks ago. It was of all the faction symbols together. Still have it?"

She stiffens. "You weren't supposed to see that."

I know why I wasn't supposed to see it, why that drawing isn't something she wants made public. It suggests leanings toward other factions instead of asserting Dauntless supremacy, like her tattoos are supposed to. Even established Dauntless members are worried about seeming Dauntless enough, and I don't know why that is, what kind of threats are leveled at people who could be called "faction traitors," but that's exactly why I'm here.

"That's sort of the point," I say. "I want that tattoo."

I thought of it on the way home, while I was cycling

through what my mother said, over and over again. *You can be more than either, more than any faction.* She thought that in order to be more than any faction, I would have to abandon this place and the people who have embraced me as their own; I would have to forgive her and let myself be swallowed by her beliefs and her lifestyle. But I don't have to leave, and I don't have to do anything I don't want to do. I can be more than any faction right here in Dauntless; maybe I already am more, and it's time to show it.

Tori looks around, her eyes jumping up to the camera in the corner, one I noticed when I walked in. She is the type who notices cameras, too.

"It was just a stupid drawing," she says loudly. "Come on, you're clearly upset—we can talk about it, find something better for you to get."

She beckons me to the back of the parlor, through the storage room behind it, and into her apartment again. We walk through the dilapidated kitchen to the living room, where her drawings are still stacked on the coffee table.

She sorts through the pages until she finds a drawing like the one I was talking about, the Dauntless flames being cupped by Abnegation hands, the Amity tree roots growing beneath an Erudite eye, which is balanced under the Candor scales. All the faction symbols stacked on top of each other. She holds it up, and I nod.

"I can't do this in a place that people will see all the time," she says. "That'll make you a walking target. A suspected faction traitor."

"I want it on my back," I say. "Covering my spine."

The hurts from my last day with my father are healed now, but I want to remember where they were; I want to remember what I escaped for as long as I live.

"You really don't do things halfway, do you." She sighs. "It'll take a long time. Several sessions. We'll have to do them in here, after hours, because I'm not going to let those cameras catch it, even if they don't bother to look in here most of the time."

"Fine," I say.

"You know, the kind of person who gets this tattoo is probably the kind that should keep it very quiet," she says, looking at me from the corner of her eye. "Or else someone will start thinking they're Divergent."

"Divergent?"

"That's a word we have for people who are aware during simulations, who refuse categorization," she says. "A word you don't speak without care, because those people often die in mysterious circumstances."

She has her elbows resting on her knees, casual, as she sketches the tattoo I want on transfer paper. Our eyes meet, and I realize: Amar. Amar was aware during simulations, and now he's dead.

Amar was Divergent.

And so am I.

"Thanks for the vocabulary lesson," I say.

"No problem." She returns to her drawing. "I'm getting the feeling you enjoy putting yourself through the wringer."

"So?" I say.

"Nothing, it's just a pretty Dauntless quality for someone who got an Abnegation result." Her mouth twitches. "Let's get started. I'll leave a note for Bud; he can jog alone just this once."

+ + +

Maybe Tori is right. Maybe I do enjoy putting myself "through the wringer"; maybe there is a masochistic streak inside me that uses pain to cope with pain. The faint burning that follows me to my next day of leadership training certainly makes it easier to focus on what I'm about to do, instead of on my mother's cold, low voice and the way I pushed her away when she tried to comfort me.

In the years after her death, I used to dream that she would come back to life in the middle of the night and run a hand over my hair and say something comforting but nonsensical, like "It will be all right" or "It will get better someday." But then I stopped allowing myself to dream, because it was more painful to long for things and never get them than to deal with whatever was in front of me. Even now I don't want to imagine what reconciling with her would be like, what having a mother would be like. I'm too old to hear comforting nonsense anymore. Too old to believe that everything will be all right.

I check the top of the bandage that protrudes over my collar to make sure it's secure. Tori outlined the first two symbols this morning, Dauntless and Abnegation, which will be larger than the others, because they are the faction I chose and the faction I actually have aptitude for, respectively—at least, I think I have aptitude for Abnegation, but it's hard to be sure. She told me to keep them covered. The Dauntless flame is the only symbol that shows with my shirt on, and I'm not in the position to remove my shirt in public very often, so I doubt that will be a problem.

Everyone else is already in the conference room, and Max is speaking to them. I feel a kind of reckless weariness as I walk through the door and take my seat. Evelyn was wrong about quite a few things, but she wasn't wrong about the Dauntless—Jeanine and Max don't want a leader of Dauntless, they want a pawn, and that's why they're selecting from the youngest of us, because young people are easier shaped and molded. I will not be molded and shaped by Jeanine Matthews. I will not be a pawn, not for them and not for my mother and not for my father; I will not belong to anyone but myself.

"Nice of you to join us," Max says. "Did this meeting interrupt your sleep?"

The others titter with laughter, and Max continues.

"As I was saying, today I would like to hear your thoughts about how to improve Dauntless—the vision you have for our faction in the coming years," he says. "I'll be meeting with you in groups by age, the oldest first. The rest of you, think of something good to say."

He leaves with the three oldest candidates. Eric is right across from me, and I notice that he has even more metal in his face than the last time I saw him—now there are rings through his eyebrows. Soon he's going to look more like a pincushion than a human being. Maybe that's the point—strategy. No one looking at him now could ever mistake him for being Erudite.

"Do my eyes deceive me, or are you really late because you were getting a tattoo?" he says, pointing to the corner of the bandage that's visible just over my shoulder.

"Lost track of time," I say. "A lot of metal appears to have attached itself to your face recently. You may want to get that checked out."

"Funny," Eric says. "Wasn't sure someone with your background could ever develop a sense of humor. Your father doesn't seem like the type to allow it."

I feel a stab of fear. He's dancing awfully close to saying my name in front of this room full of people, and he wants me to know it—he wants me to remember that he knows who I am, and that he can use it against me whenever he pleases.

I can't pretend that it doesn't matter to me. The power dynamic has shifted, and I can't make it shift back.

"I think I know who told you that," I say. Jeanine Matthews knows both my name and my alias. She must have given him both.

"I was already fairly sure," he says in a low voice. "But my suspicions were confirmed by a credible source, yes. You aren't as good at keeping secrets as you think, Four."

I would threaten him, tell him that if he reveals my name to the Dauntless, I'll reveal his lasting connections to Erudite. But I don't have any evidence, and the Dauntless dislike Abnegation more than Erudite anyway. I sit back in my chair to wait.

The others file out as they're called, and soon we're the only ones left. Max makes his way down the hallway, then beckons to us from the door, without a word. We follow him back to his office, which I recognize from yesterday's footage of his meeting with Jeanine Matthews. I use my memory of that conversation to steel myself against what's coming next.

"So." Max folds his hands on his desk, and again I'm struck by how strange it is to see him in such a clean, formal environment. He belongs in a training room, hitting a bag, or next to the Pit, leaning over the railing. Not sitting at a low wooden table surrounded by paper.

I look out the windows of the Pire at the Dauntless sector of the city. A few yards away I can see the edge of the hole I jumped into when I first chose Dauntless, and the rooftop that I stood on just before that. *I chose Dauntless*, I told my mother yesterday. *That's where I belong.*

Is that really true?

"Eric, let's begin with you," Max says. "Do you have ideas for what might be good for Dauntless, moving forward?"

"I do." Eric sits up. "I think we need to make some changes, and I think they should start during initiation."

"What kind of changes do you have in mind?"

"Dauntless has always embraced a spirit of competition," Eric says. "Competition makes us better; it brings out the best, strongest parts of us. I think initiation should foster that sense of competition more than it currently does, so that it produces the best initiates possible. Right now initiates are competing only against the system, striving for a particular score in order to move forward. I think they should be competing against each other for spots in Dauntless."

I can't help it; I turn and stare at him. A limited number of spots? In a faction? After just *two weeks* of initiation training?

"And if they don't get a spot?"

"They become factionless," Eric says. I swallow a derisive laugh. Eric continues, "If we believe that Dauntless truly is the superior faction to join, that its aims are more important than the aims of other factions, then becoming one of us should be an honor and a privilege, not a right."

"Are you kidding?" I say, unable to contain myself any longer. "People choose a faction because they value the same things that faction values, not because they're already proficient in what a faction teaches. You'd be kicking people out of Dauntless just for not being strong enough to jump on a train or win a fight. You would favor the big, strong, and reckless more than the small, smart, and brave—you wouldn't be improving Dauntless at all."

"I'm sure the small, smart ones would be better off in Erudite, or as little gray-clad Stiffs," Eric says with a wry smile. "And I don't think you're giving our potential new Dauntless members enough credit, Four. This system would favor only the most determined."

I glance at Max. I expect him to look unimpressed by Eric's plan, but he doesn't. He's leaning forward, focused on Eric's pierced face like something about it has inspired him.

"This is an interesting debate," Max says. "Four, how would you improve Dauntless, if not by making initiation more competitive?"

I shake my head, looking out the window again. *You aren't one of those mindless, danger-seeking fools,* my mother said to me. But those are the people Eric wants in Dauntless: mindless, danger-seeking fools. If Eric is one of Jeanine Matthew's lackeys, then why would Jeanine encourage him to propose this kind of plan?

Oh. Because mindless, danger-seeking fools are easier to control, easier to manipulate. Obviously.

"I would improve Dauntless by fostering true bravery instead of stupidity and brutality," I say. "Take out the knife throwing. Prepare people physically and mentally to defend the weak against the strong. That's what our manifesto encourages—ordinary acts of bravery. I think we should return to that."

"And then we can all hold hands and sing a song together, right?" Eric rolls his eyes. "You want to turn Dauntless into Amity."

"No," I say. "I want to make sure we still know how to think for ourselves, think about more than the next surge of adrenaline. Or just think, period. That way we can't be taken over or . . . controlled from the outside."

"Sounds a little Erudite to me," Eric says.

"The ability to think isn't exclusive to Erudite," I snap. "The ability to think in stressful situations is what the fear simulations are supposed to develop."

"All right, all right," Max says, holding up his hands. He looks troubled. "Four, I'm sorry to say this, but you sound a little paranoid. Who would take us over, or try to control us? The factions have coexisted peacefully for longer than you've been alive, there's no reason that's going to change now."

I open my mouth to tell him he's wrong, that the second he let Jeanine Matthews get involved in the affairs of our faction, the second he let her plant Erudite-loyal transfers into our initiation program, the second he started consulting with her on who to appoint as the next Dauntless leader, he compromised the system of checks and balances that has allowed us to coexist peacefully for so long. But then I realize that to tell him those things would be to accuse him of treason, and to reveal just how much I know.

Max looks at me, and I read disappointment in his face.

I know that he likes me—likes me more than Eric, at least. But my mother was right yesterday—Max doesn't want someone like me, someone who can think for himself, develop his own agenda. He wants someone like Eric, who will help him establish the new Dauntless agenda, who will be easy to manipulate simply because he's still under the thumb of Jeanine Matthews, someone with whom Max is closely aligned.

My mother presented me with two options yesterday: be a pawn of Dauntless, or become factionless. But there's a third option: to be neither. To align myself with no one in particular. To live under the radar, and free. That's what I really want—to shed all the people who want to form and shape me, one by one, and learn instead to form and shape myself.

"To be honest, sir, I don't think this is the right place for me," I say calmly. "I told you when you first asked me that I'd like to be an instructor, and I think I'm realizing more and more that that's where I belong."

"Eric, will you excuse us, please?" Max says. Eric, barely able to suppress his glee, nods and leaves. I don't watch him go, but I would bet all my Dauntless credits that there's a little skip in his step as he walks down the hallway.

Max gets up and sits next to me, in the chair Eric just vacated.

"I hope you're not saying this because I accused you of being paranoid," Max says. "I was just concerned about you. I feared that the pressure was getting to you, making you stop thinking straight. I still think you're a strong candidate for leadership. You fit the right profile, you've demonstrated proficiency with everything we've taught you—and beyond that, quite frankly, you're more likable than some of our other promising candidates, which is important in a close working environment."

"Thank you," I say. "But you're right, the pressure is getting to me. And the pressure if I was actually a leader would be much worse."

Max nods sadly. "Well." He nods again. "If you'd like to be an initiation instructor, I will arrange that for you. But that's seasonal work—where would you like to be placed for the rest of the year?"

"I was thinking maybe the control room," I say. "I've discovered that I enjoy working with computers. I don't think I would enjoy patrolling nearly as much."

"Okay," Max says. "Consider it done. Thank you for being honest with me."

I get up, and all I feel is relief. He seems concerned,

sympathetic. Not suspicious of me or my motives or my paranoia.

"If you ever change your mind," Max says, "please don't hesitate to tell me. We could always use someone like you."

"Thank you," I say, and even though he's the worst faction traitor of anyone I've met, and probably responsible at least in part for Amar's death, I can't help but feel a little grateful to him for letting me go so easily.

+ + +

Eric is waiting for me around the corner. As I try to walk past him, he grabs my arm.

"Careful, Eaton," he murmurs. "If anything about my involvement with Erudite escapes you, you won't like what happens to you."

"You won't like what happens to you, either, if you ever call me by that name again."

"Soon I'm going to be one of your leaders," Eric says, smirking. "And believe me, I am going to keep a very, very close eye on you and how well you implement my new training methods."

"He doesn't like you, you know that?" I say. "Max, I mean. He'd rather have anyone else but you. He's not going to give you more than an inch in any direction. So good luck with your short leash."

I wrench my arm from his grasp and walk toward the elevators.

+++

"Man," Shauna says. "That *is* a bad day."

"Yeah."

She and I are sitting next to the chasm with our feet over the edge. I rest my head against the bars of the metal barrier that's keeping us from falling to our deaths, and feel the spray of water against my ankles as one of the larger waves hits a wall.

I told her about my departure from leadership training, and Eric's threat, but I didn't tell her about my mother. How do you tell someone that your mother came back from the dead?

All my life, someone has been trying to control me. Marcus was the tyrant of our house, and nothing happened without his permission. And then Max wanted to recruit me as his Dauntless yes-man. And even my mother had a plan for me, for me to join up with her when I reached a certain age to work against the faction system that *she* has a vendetta against, for whatever reason. And just when I thought that I had escaped control altogether, Eric swooped in to remind me that if he became a

Dauntless leader, he would be watching me.

All I have, I realize, are the small moments of rebellion I'm able to manage, just like when I was in Abnegation, collecting objects I found on the street. The tattoo that Tori is drawing on my back, the one that might declare me to be Divergent, is one of those moments. I'll have to keep looking for more of them, more brief moments of freedom in a world that refuses to allow it.

"Where's Zeke?" I say.

"I don't know," she says. "I haven't wanted to hang out with him much recently."

I look sideways at her. "You could just tell him that you like him, you know. I honestly don't think he has a clue."

"That's obvious," she says, snorting. "But what if this is what he wants—to just bounce around from girl to girl for a while? I don't want to be one of those girls he bounces to."

"I seriously doubt you would be," I say, "but fair enough."

We sit quietly for a few seconds, both of us staring down at the raging water below.

"You'll be a good instructor," she says. "You were really good at teaching me."

"Thanks."

"*There* you are," Zeke says from behind us. He's carrying a large bottle full of some kind of brown liquid, holding it by the neck. "Come on. I found something."

Shauna and I look at each other and shrug, then follow him to the doors on the other side of the Pit, the ones we first went through after jumping into the net. But instead of leading us toward the net, he takes us through another door—the lock is taped down with duct tape—and down a pitch-black corridor and a flight of stairs.

"Should be coming up—ouch!"

"Sorry, I didn't know you were stopping," Shauna says.

"Hold on, almost got it—"

He opens a door, letting faint light in so we can see where we are. We're on the other side of the chasm, several feet above the water. Above us, the Pit seems to go on forever, and the people milling around near the railing are small and dark, impossible to distinguish from this distance.

I laugh. Zeke just led us into another small moment of rebellion, probably without meaning to.

"How did you *find* this place?" Shauna says with obvious wonder as she jumps down onto one of the lower rocks. Now that I'm here, I see a path that would carry us up and across the wall, if we wanted to walk to the other side of the chasm.

"That girl Maria," Zeke says. "Her mom works in chasm maintenance. I didn't know there was such a thing, but apparently there is."

"You still seeing her?" Shauna asks, trying to be casual.

"Nah," Zeke says. "Every time I was with her I just kept getting the itch to be with friends instead. That's not a good sign, right?"

"No," Shauna agrees, and she seems more cheerful than before.

I lower myself more carefully onto the rock Shauna is standing on. Zeke sits next to her, opening his bottle and passing it around.

"I heard you're out of the running," Zeke says when he passes it to me. "Thought you might need a drink."

"Yeah," I say, and then I take a swig.

"Consider this act of public drunkenness a big—" He makes an obscene gesture toward the glass ceiling above the Pit. "You know, to Max and Eric."

And Evelyn, I think, as I take another swallow.

"I'll be working in the control room when I'm not training initiates," I say.

"Awesome," Zeke says. "It'll be good to have a friend in

there. Right now no one talks to me."

"Sounds like me in my old faction," I say with a laugh. "Imagine an entire lunch period in which no one even looks at you."

"Ouch," Zeke says. "Well, I bet you're glad to be here now, then."

I take the bottle from him again, drink another mouthful of stinging, burning alcohol, and wipe my mouth with the back of my hand. "Yeah," I say. "I am."

If the factions are deteriorating, as my mother would have me believe, this is not a bad place to watch them fall apart. At least here I have friends to keep me company while it happens.

+ + +

It's just after dark, and I have my hood up to hide my face as I run through the factionless area of the city, right by the border it shares with the Abnegation sector. I had to go to the school to get my bearings, but now I remember where I am, and where I ran, that day that I barged into a factionless warehouse in search of a dying ember.

I reach the door I walked through when I exited, and tap on it with my first knuckle. I can hear voices just beyond it and smell food coming from one of the open windows, where smoke from the fire within is leaking into the alley. Footsteps, as someone comes to see what the knocking is about.

This time the man is wearing a red Amity shirt and black Dauntless pants. He still has a towel tucked into his back pocket, the same as the last time I spoke to him. He opens the door just enough to look at me, and no farther.

"Well, look who made a change," he said, eyeing my Dauntless clothes. "To what do I owe this visit? Did you miss my charming company?"

"You knew my mother was alive when you met me," I say. "That's how you recognized me, because you've spent time with her. That's how you knew what she said about inertia carrying her to Abnegation."

"Yeah," the man said. "Didn't think it was my business to be the one to tell you she was still alive. You here to demand an apology, or something?"

"No," I say. "I'm here to hand off a message. You'll give it to her?"

"Yeah, sure. I'll be seeing her in the next couple days."

I reach into my pocket and take out a folded piece of paper. I offer it to him.

"Go ahead and read it, I don't care," I say. "And thanks."

"No problem," he says. "Want to come in? You're starting to seem more like one of us than one of them, Eaton."

I shake my head.

I make my way back down the alley, and before I turn the corner, I see him opening up the note to read what it says.

> *Evelyn,*
> *Someday. Not yet.*
> *—4*
> *P.S. I'm glad you're not dead.*

THE TRAITOR

ANOTHER YEAR, ANOTHER Visiting Day.

Two years ago, when I was an initiate, I pretended my own Visiting Day didn't exist, holed up in the training room with a punching bag. I was there for so long that I smelled the dust-sweat for days afterward. Last year, the first year I taught initiates, I did the same thing, though Zeke and Shauna both invited me to spend the day with their families instead.

This year I have more important things to do than punch a bag and mope about my family dysfunction. I'm going to the control room.

I walk through the Pit, dodging tearful reunions and shrieks of laughter. Families can always come together on Visiting Day, even if they're from different factions, but over time, they usually stop coming. "Faction before blood," after all. Most of the mixed clothing I see belongs to transfer families: Will's Erudite sister is dressed in light blue, Peter's Candor parents are in black and white. For a moment I watch his parents, and wonder if they made him into the person he is. But most of the time, people aren't that easy to explain, I guess.

I'm supposed to be on a mission, but I pause next to the chasm, pressing into the railing. Bits of paper float in the water. Now that I know where the steps cut into the stone in the opposite wall are, I can see them right away, and the hidden doorway that leads to them. I smile a little, thinking of the nights I've spent on those rocks with Zeke or Shauna, sometimes talking and sometimes just sitting and listening to the water move.

I hear footsteps approaching, and look over my shoulder. Tris is walking toward me, tucked under the gray-clad arm of an Abnegation woman. Natalie Prior. I stiffen, suddenly desperate to escape—what if Natalie knows who I am, where I came from? What if she lets it slip, here, surrounded by all these people?

She can't possibly recognize me. I don't look anything like the boy she knew, lanky and slouched and buried in fabric.

When she's close enough, she extends her hand. "Hello,

my name is Natalie. I'm Beatrice's mother."

Beatrice. That name is so wrong for her.

I clasp Natalie's hand and shake it. I've never been fond of Dauntless hand-shaking. It's too unpredictable—you never know how tightly to squeeze, how many times to shake.

"Four," I say. "It's nice to meet you."

"Four," Natalie says, and she smiles. "Is that a nickname?"

"Yes," I say. I change the subject. "Your daughter is doing well here. I've been overseeing her training."

"That's good to hear," she says. "I know a few things about Dauntless initiation, and I was worried about her."

I glance at Tris. There's color in her cheeks—she looks happy, like seeing her mother is doing her some good. For the first time I fully appreciate how much she's changed since I first saw her, tumbling onto the wooden platform, fragile-looking, like the impact with the net should have shattered her. She doesn't look fragile anymore, with the shadows of bruises on her face and a new stability in the way she stands, like she's ready for anything.

"You shouldn't worry," I say to Natalie.

Tris looks away. I think she's still angry with me for the way I nicked her ear with that knife. I guess I don't really blame her.

"You look familiar for some reason, Four," Natalie says. I would think her comment was lighthearted if not for the way she's looking at me, like she's pinning me down.

"I can't imagine why," I say, as coldly as I can manage. "I don't make a habit of associating with the Abnegation."

She doesn't react the way I expect her to, with surprise or fear or anger. She just laughs. "Few people do, these days. I don't take it personally."

If she does recognize me, she doesn't seem eager to say so. I try to relax.

"Well, I'll leave you to your reunion," I say.

+ + +

On my screen, the security footage switches from the lobby of the Pire to the hole hemmed in by four buildings, the initiate entrance to Dauntless. A crowd is gathered around the hole, climbing in and out of it, I assume to test the net.

"Not into Visiting Day?" My supervisor, Gus, stands at my shoulder, sipping from a mug of coffee. He's not that old, but there's a bald spot at the crown of his head. He keeps the rest of his hair short, even shorter than mine. His earlobes are stretched around wide discs. "I didn't think I'd see you again until initiation was over."

"Figured I might as well do something productive."

On my screen, everyone crawls out of the hole and

stands aside, their backs against one of the buildings. A dark figure inches toward the edge of the roof high above the hole, runs a few steps, and jumps off. My stomach drops like I'm the one falling, and the figure disappears beneath the pavement. I'll never get used to seeing that.

"They seem to be having a good time," Gus says, sipping his coffee again. "Well, you're always welcome to work when you're not scheduled to, but it's not a crime to go have some mindless fun, Four."

He walks away, and I mumble, "So I'm told."

I look over the control room. It's almost empty—on Visiting Day, only a few people are required to work, and it's usually the oldest ones. Gus is hunched over his screen. Two others flank him, scanning through footage with their headphones half on, half off. And then there's me.

I type in a command, calling up the footage I saved last week. It shows Max in his office, sitting at his computer. He pokes at the keys with an index finger, hunting for the right ones for several seconds between jabs. Not many of the Dauntless know how to type properly, especially Max, who I'm told spent most of his Dauntless time patrolling the factionless sector with a gun at his side—he must not have anticipated that he would ever need to use a computer. I lean close to the screen to make sure that the numbers I took down earlier are accurate. If they are, I have Max's account password written on a piece of paper in my pocket.

Ever since I realized that Max was working closely with Jeanine Matthews, and began to suspect that they had something to do with Amar's death, I've been looking for a way to investigate further. When I saw him type in his password the other day, I found one.

084628. Yes, the numbers look right. I call up the live security footage again, and cycle through the camera feeds until I find the ones that show Max's office and the hallway beyond it. Then I type the command to take the footage of Max's office out of the rotation, so Gus and the others won't see it; it will only play on my screen. The footage from the whole city is always divided by however many people are in the control room, so we aren't all looking at the same feeds. We're only supposed to pull footage from the general rotation like that for a few seconds at a time, if we need a closer look at something, but hopefully this won't take me long. I slip out of the room and walk toward the elevators.

This level of the Pire is almost empty—everyone is gone. That will make it easier for me to do what I have to do. I ride the elevator up to the tenth floor, and walk purposefully toward Max's office. I've found that when you're sneaking around, it's best not to look like you're sneaking around. I tap the flash drive in my pocket as I walk, and turn the corner toward Max's office.

I nudge the door open with my shoe—earlier today, after I was sure he had gone to the Pit to start Visiting Day preparations, I'd crept up here and taped the lock. I close the door quietly behind me, not turning on the lights, and crouch next to his desk. I don't want to move the chair to sit in it; I don't want him to see that anything about this room has changed when he gets back.

The screen prompts me for a password. My mouth feels dry. I take the paper from my pocket and press it flat to the desk top while I type it in. 084628.

The screen shifts. I can't believe it worked.

Hurry. If Gus discovers that I'm gone, that I'm in here, I don't know what I'll say, what excuse I could possibly give that would sound reasonable. I insert the flash drive and transfer the program I put there earlier. I asked Lauren, one of the Dauntless technical staff and my fellow initiation instructor, for a program that would make one computer mirror another, under the pretense that I wanted to prank Zeke when we're at work. She was happy to help—another thing I've discovered is that the Dauntless are always up for a prank, and rarely looking for a lie.

With a few simple keystrokes, the program is installed

and buried somewhere in Max's computer that I'm sure he would never bother to access. I put the flash drive back in my pocket, along with the piece of paper with his password on it, and leave the office without getting my fingerprints on the glass part of the door.

That was easy, I think, as I walk toward the elevators again. According to my watch, it only took me five minutes. I can claim that I was on a bathroom break if anyone asks.

But when I get back to the control room, Gus is standing at my computer, staring at my screen.

I freeze. How long has he been there? Did he see me break into Max's office?

"Four," Gus says, sounding grave. "Why did you isolate this footage? You're not supposed to take feeds out of rotation, you know that."

"I . . ." *Lie! Lie now!* "I thought I saw something," I finish lamely. "We're allowed to isolate footage if we see something out of the ordinary."

Gus moves toward me.

"So," he says, "then why did I just see you on this screen coming out of that same hallway?"

He points to the hallway on my screen. My throat tightens.

"I thought I saw something, and I went upstairs to

investigate it," I say. "I'm sorry, I just wanted to move around."

He stares at me, chewing the inside of his cheek. I don't move. I don't look away.

"If you ever see something out of the ordinary again, you follow the protocol. You report it to your supervisor, who is . . . who, again?"

"You," I say, sighing a little. I don't like to be patronized.

"Correct. I see you *can* keep up," he says. "Honestly, Four, after over a year of working here there shouldn't be so many irregularities in your job performance. We have very clear rules, and all you have to do is follow them. This is your last warning. Okay?"

"Okay," I say. I've been chastised a few times for pulling feeds out of rotation to watch meetings with Jeanine Matthews and Max, or with Max and Eric. It never gave me any useful information, and I almost always got caught.

"Good." His voice lightens up a little. "Good luck with the initiates. You got transfers again this year?"

"Yeah," I say. "Lauren gets the Dauntless-borns."

"Ah, too bad. I was hoping you would get to know my little sister," Gus says. "If I were you, I'd go do something to wind down. We're fine in here. Just let that footage loose before you go."

He walks back to his computer, and I unclench my jaw. I wasn't even aware that I was doing it. My face throbbing, I shut down my computer and leave the control room. I can't believe I got away with it.

Now, with this program installed on Max's computer, I can go through every single one of his files from the relative privacy of the control room. I can find out exactly what he and Jeanine Matthews are up to.

+ + +

That night I dream that I'm walking through the hallways of the Pire, and I'm alone, but the corridors don't end, and the view from the windows doesn't change, lofted train tracks curving into tall buildings, the sun buried in clouds. I feel like I'm walking for hours, and when I wake with a start, it's like I never slept at all.

Then I hear a knock, and a voice shouting, "Open up!"

This feels more like a nightmare than the tedium I just escaped—I'm sure it's Dauntless soldiers coming to my door because they found out I'm Divergent, or that I'm spying on Max, or that I've been in touch with my faction- less mother in the past year. All things that say "faction traitor."

Dauntless soldiers coming to kill me—but as I walk to the door, I realize that if they were going to do that, they wouldn't make so much noise in the hallway. And besides, that's Zeke's voice.

"Zeke," I say when I open the door. "What's your problem? It's the middle of the night."

There's a line of sweat on his forehead, and he's out of breath. He must have run here.

"I was working the night shift in the control room," Zeke says. "Something happened in the transfer dorm."

For some reason, my first thought is *her*, her wide eyes staring at me from the recesses of my memory.

"What?" I say. "To who?"

"Walk and talk," Zeke says.

I put on my shoes and pull on my jacket and follow him down the hall.

"The Erudite guy. Blond," Zeke says.

I have to suppress a sigh of relief. It's not her. Nothing happened to her. "Will?"

"No, the other one."

"Edward."

"Yeah, Edward. He was attacked. Stabbed."

"Dead?"

"Alive. Got hit in the eye."

I stop. "In the *eye*?"

Zeke nods.

"Who did you tell?"

"Night supervisor. He went to tell Eric, Eric said he would handle it."

"Sure he will." I veer to the right, away from the transfer dormitory.

"Where are you going?" Zeke says.

"Edward's already in the infirmary?" I walk backward as I talk.

Zeke nods.

I say, "Then I'm going to see Max."

+ + +

The Dauntless compound isn't so large that I don't know where people live. Max's apartment is buried deep in the underground corridors of the compound, near a back door that opens up right next to the train tracks outside. I march toward it, following the blue emergency lamps run by our solar generator.

I pound on the metal door with my fist, waking Max the same way Zeke woke me. He yanks the door open a few seconds later, his feet bare and his eyes wild.

"What happened?" he says.

"One of my initiates was stabbed in the eye," I say.

"And you came here? Didn't someone inform Eric?"

"Yeah. That's what I want to talk to you about. Mind if I come in?"

I don't wait for an answer—I brush past him and walk into his living room. He flips on the lights, displaying the messiest living space I've ever seen, used cups and plates strewn across the coffee table, all the couch cushions in disarray, the floor gray with dust.

"I want initiation to go back to what it was before Eric made it more competitive," I say, "and I want him out of my training room."

"You don't really think it's Eric's fault that an initiate got hurt," Max says, crossing his arms. "Or that you're in any position to make demands."

"Yes, it's his fault, of course it's his fault!" I say, louder than I mean to be. "If they weren't all fighting for one of ten slots, they wouldn't be so desperate they're ready to attack each other! He has them wound up so tight, of course they're bound to explode eventually!"

Max is quiet. He looks annoyed, but he isn't calling me ridiculous, which is a start.

"You don't think the initiate who did the attacking should be held responsible?" Max says. "You don't think he or she is the one to blame, instead of Eric?"

"Of course he—she—whoever—should be held responsible," I say. "But this never would have happened if Eric—"

"You can't say that with any certainty," Max says.

"I can say it with the certainty of a reasonable person."

"I'm not reasonable?" His voice is low, dangerous, and suddenly I remember that Max is not just the Dauntless leader who likes me for some inexplicable reason—he's the Dauntless leader who's working closely with Jeanine Matthews, the one who appointed Eric, the one who probably had something to do with Amar's death.

"That's not what I meant," I say, trying to stay calm.

"You should be careful to communicate exactly what you mean," Max says, moving closer to me. "Or someone will start to think you're insulting your superiors."

I don't respond. He moves still closer.

"Or questioning the values of your faction," he says, and his bloodshot eyes drift to my shoulder, where the Dauntless flames of my tattoo stick out over the collar of my shirt. I have hidden the five faction symbols that cover my spine since I got them, but for some reason, at this moment, I am terrified that Max knows about them. Knows what they mean, which is that I am not a perfect Dauntless member; I am someone who believes that more than one virtue should be prized; I am Divergent.

"You had your shot to become a Dauntless leader," Max says. "Maybe you could have avoided this incident had you not backed out like a coward. But you did. So now you have to deal with the consequences."

His face is showing his age. It has lines it didn't have

last year, or the year before, and his skin is grayish brown, like it was dusted with ash.

"Eric is as involved in initiation as he is because you refused to follow orders last year—" Last year, in the training room, I stopped all the fights before the injuries became too severe, against Eric's command that the fighting only stop when one person was unable to continue. I nearly lost my position as initiation instructor as a result; I would have, if Max hadn't gotten involved.

"—and I wanted to give you another chance to make it right, with closer monitoring," Max says. "You're failing to do so. You've gone too far."

The sweat I worked up on my way here has turned cold. He steps back and opens his door again.

"Get out of my apartment and deal with your initiates," Max says. "Don't let me see you step out of line again."

"Yes, sir," I say quietly, and I leave.

+++

I go to see Edward in the infirmary early in the morning, when the sun is rising, shining through the glass ceiling of the Pit. His head is wrapped in white bandages, and he's not moving, not speaking. I don't say anything to him, just sit by his head and watch the minutes tick by on the wall clock.

I've been an idiot. I thought I was invincible, that Max's desire to have me as a fellow leader would never waver, that on some level he trusted me. I should have known better. All Max ever wanted was a pawn—that's what my mother said.

I can't be a pawn. But I'm not sure what I should be instead.

+ + +

The setting Tris Prior invents is eerie and almost beautiful, the sky yellow-green, yellow grass stretching for miles in every direction.

Watching someone else's fear simulation is strange. Intimate. I don't feel right about forcing other people to be vulnerable, even if I don't like them. Every human being is entitled to her secrets. Watching my initiates' fears, one after another, makes me feel like my skin has been scraped raw with sandpaper.

In Tris's simulation, the yellow grass is perfectly still. If the air wasn't stagnant, I would say this was a dream, not a nightmare—but still air means only one thing to me, and that is a coming storm.

A shadow moves across the grass, and a large black bird lands on her shoulder, curling its talons into her shirt. My fingertips prickle, remembering how I touched her shoulder when she walked into the simulation room, how I brushed her hair away from her neck to inject her. Stupid. Careless.

She hits the black bird, hard, and then everything happens at once. Thunder rumbles; the sky darkens, not with storm clouds, but with *birds*, an impossibly huge swarm of them, moving in unison like many parts of the same mind.

The sound of her scream is the worst sound in the world, desperate—she's desperate for help and I am desperate to help her, though I know what I'm seeing isn't real, I know it. The crows keep coming, relentless, surrounding her, burying her alive in dark feathers. She screams for help and I can't help her and I don't want to watch this, I don't want to watch another second.

But then, she starts to move, shifting so she's lying in the grass, relenting, relaxing. If she's in pain now she doesn't show it; she just closes her eyes and surrenders, and that is worse than her screaming for help, somehow.

Then it's over.

She lurches forward in the metal chair, smacking at her body to get the birds off, though they're gone. Then she curls into a ball and hides her face.

I reach out to touch her shoulder, to reassure her, and she hits my arm, hard. "Don't touch me!"

"It's over," I say, wincing—she punches harder than she realizes. I ignore the pain and run a hand over her hair, because I'm stupid, and inappropriate, and stupid . . .

"Tris."

She just shifts back and forth, soothing herself.

"Tris, I'm going to take you back to the dorms, okay?"

"No! They can't see me . . . not like this. . . ."

This is what Eric's new system creates: A brave human being has just defeated one of her worst fears in less than five minutes, an ordeal that takes most people at least twice that time, but she's terrified to go back into the hallway, to be seen as weak or vulnerable in any way. Tris is Dauntless, plain and simple, but this faction isn't really Dauntless anymore.

"Oh, calm down," I say, more irritable than I mean to be. "I'll take you out the back door."

"I don't need you to . . ." I can see her hands trembling even as she shrugs off my offer.

"Nonsense," I say. I take her arm and help her to her feet. She wipes her eyes as I move toward the back door. Amar once took me through this door, tried to walk me back to the dormitory even when I didn't want him to, the way she probably doesn't want me to now. How is it possible to live the same story twice, from different vantage points?

She yanks her arm from mine, and turns on me. "Why

did you do that to me? What was the point of that, huh? I wasn't aware that when I chose Dauntless, I was signing up for weeks of torture!"

If she was anyone else, any of the other initiates, I would have yelled at her for insubordination a dozen times by now. I would have felt threatened by her constant assaults against my character, and tried to squelch her uprisings with cruelty, the way I did to Christina on the first day of initiation. But Tris earned my respect when she jumped first, into the net; when she challenged me at her first meal; when she wasn't deterred by my unpleasant responses to questions; when she spoke up for Al and stared me right in the eye as I threw knives at her. She's not my subordinate, couldn't possibly be.

"Did you think overcoming cowardice would be easy?" I say.

"That isn't overcoming cowardice! Cowardice is how you decide to be in real life, and in real life, I am not getting pecked to death by crows, Four!"

She starts to cry, but I'm too struck by what she just said to feel uncomfortable with her tears. She's not learning the lessons Eric wants her to learn. She's learning different things, wiser ones.

"I want to go home," she says.

I know where the cameras are in this hallway. I hope

none of them have picked up on what she just said.

"Learning how to think in the midst of fear is a lesson that everyone, even your Stiff family, needs to learn," I say. I doubt a lot of things about Dauntless initiation, but the fear simulations aren't one of them; they are the most straightforward way for a person to engage their own fears and conquer them, far more straightforward than the knife throwing or the fighting. "That's what we're trying to teach you. If you can't learn it, you'll need to get the hell out of here, because we won't want you."

I'm hard on her because I know she can handle it. And also because I don't know any other way to be.

"I'm trying. But I failed. I'm failing."

I almost feel like laughing. "How long do you think you spent in that hallucination, Tris?"

"I don't know. A half hour?"

"Three minutes," I say. "You got out three times faster than any of the other initiates. Whatever you are, you're not a failure."

You might be Divergent, I think. But she didn't do anything to change the simulation, so maybe she's not. Maybe she's just that brave.

I smile at her. "Tomorrow you'll be better at this. You'll see."

"Tomorrow?"

She's calmer now. I touch her back, right beneath her shoulders.

"What was your first hallucination?" she asks me.

"It wasn't a 'what' so much as a 'who.'" As I'm saying it, I think I should have just told her the first obstacle in my fear landscape, fear of heights, though it's not exactly what she's asking about. When I'm around her I can't control what I say the way I do around other people. I say vague things because that's as close as I can get to stopping myself from saying anything, my mind addled by the feeling of her body through her shirt. "It's not important."

"And are you over that fear now?"

"Not yet." We're at the dormitory door. The walk has never gone by so quickly. I put my hands in my pockets so I don't do anything stupid with them again. "I may never be."

"So they don't go away?"

"Sometimes they do. And sometimes new fears replace them. But becoming fearless isn't the point. That's impossible. It's learning how to control your fear, and how to be free from it, *that's* the point."

She nods. I don't know what she came here for, but if I had to guess, it would be that she chose Dauntless for its freedom. Abnegation would have stifled the spark in her until it died out. Dauntless, for all its faults, has kindled the spark into a flame.

"Anyway," I say. "Your fears are rarely what they appear to be in the simulation."

"What do you mean?"

"Well, are you really afraid of crows?" I grin. "When you see one, do you run away screaming?"

"No, I guess not."

She moves closer to me. I felt safer when there was more space between us. Even closer, and I think about touching her, and my mouth goes dry. I almost never think about people that way, about girls that way.

"So what am I really afraid of?" she says.

"I don't know," I say. "Only you can know."

"I didn't know Dauntless would be this difficult."

I'm glad to have something else to think about, other than how easy it would be to fit my hand to the arch of her back.

"It wasn't always like this, I'm told. Being Dauntless, I mean."

"What changed?"

"The leadership. The person who controls training sets the standard of Dauntless behavior. Six years ago Max and the other leaders changed the training methods to make them more competitive and more brutal." Six years ago, the combat portion of training was brief and didn't include bare-knuckled sparring. Initiates wore padding. The emphasis was on being strong and capable, and on developing camaraderie with the other initiates. And even when I was an initiate, it was better than this—an unlimited potential for initiates to become members, fights that stopped when one person conceded. "Said it was to test people's strength. And that changed the priorities of Dauntless as a whole. Bet you can't guess who the leaders' new protégé is."

Of course, she does immediately. "So if you were ranked first in your initiate class, what was Eric's rank?"

"Second."

"So he was their second choice for leadership. And you were their first."

Perceptive. I don't know that I was the first choice, but I was certainly a better option than Eric. "What makes you say that?"

"The way Eric was acting at dinner the first night. Jealous, even though he has what he wants."

I've never thought of Eric that way. Jealous? Of what? I've never taken anything from him, never posed a real threat to him. He's the one who came after Amar, who came after me. But maybe she's right—maybe I never saw how frustrated he was to be second to a transfer from Abnegation, after all his hard work, or that I was favored by Max for leadership even when he was positioned here specifically to take the leadership role.

She wipes her face.

"Do I look like I've been crying?"

The question seems almost funny to me. Her tears vanished almost as quickly as they came, and now her face is fair again, her eyes dry, her hair smooth. Like nothing ever happened—like she didn't just spend three minutes overwhelmed by terror. She's stronger than I was.

"Hmm." I lean in closer, making a joke of examining her, but then it's not a joke, and I'm just close, and we're sharing a breath.

"No, Tris," I say. "You look . . ." I try a Dauntless expression. "Tough as nails."

She smiles a little. So do I.

+ + +

"Hey," Zeke says sleepily, leaning his head into his fist. "Want to take over for me? I practically need to tape my eyes open."

"Sorry," I say. "I just need to use a computer. You do know it's only nine o'clock, right?"

He yawns. "I get tired when I'm bored out of my mind. Shift's almost over, though."

I love the control room at night. There are only three people monitoring the footage, so the room is silent except for the hum of computers. Through the windows I see only a sliver of the moon; everything else is dark. It's hard to find peace in the Dauntless compound, and this is the place where I find it most often.

Zeke turns back to his screen. I sit at a computer a few seats over from him, and angle the screen away from the room. Then I log in, using the fake account name I set up several months ago, so no one would be able to track this back to me.

Once I'm logged in, I open the mirroring program that lets me use Max's computer remotely. It takes a second to kick in, but when it does, it's like I'm sitting in Max's office, using the same machine he uses.

I work quickly, systematically. He labels his folders with numbers, so I don't know what each one will contain. Most are benign, lists of Dauntless members or schedules of events. I open them and close them in seconds.

I go deeper into the files, folder after folder, and then I find something strange. A list of supplies, but the supplies don't involve food or fabric or anything else I would expect for mundane Dauntless life—the list is for weapons. Syringes. And something marked *Serum D2*.

I can imagine only one thing that would require the Dauntless to have so many weapons: an attack. But on who?

I check the control room again, my heartbeat pounding in my head. Zeke is playing a computer game that he wrote himself. The second control-room operator is slumped to one side, her eyes half-closed. The third is stirring his glass of water idly with his straw, staring out the windows. No one is paying attention to me.

I open more files. After a few wasted efforts, I find a map. It's marked mostly with letters and numbers, so at first I don't know what it's showing.

Then I open a map of the city on the Dauntless database to compare them, and sit back in my chair as I realize what streets Max's map is focusing on.

The Abnegation sector.

The attack will be against Abnegation.

+ + +

It should have been obvious, of course. Who else would Max and Jeanine bother to attack? Max and Jeanine's vendetta is against Abnegation, and it always has been. I should have realized that when the Erudite released that story about my father, the monstrous husband and father. The only true thing they've written, as far as I can tell.

Zeke nudges my leg with his foot. "Shift's over. Bedtime?"

"No," I say. "I need a drink."

He perks up noticeably. It's not every night I decide I want to abandon my sterile, withdrawn existence for an evening of Dauntless indulgence.

"I'm your man," he says.

I close down the program, my account, everything. I try to leave the information about the Abnegation attack behind, too, until I can figure out what to do about it, but it chases me all the way into the elevator, through the lobby, and down the paths to the bottom of the Pit.

+ + +

I surface from the simulation with a heavy feeling in the pit of my stomach. I detach from the wires and get up. She's still recovering from the sensation of almost drowning, shaking her hands and taking deep breaths. I watch her for a moment, not sure how to say what I need to say.

"What?" she says.

"How did you do that?"

"Do what?"

"Crack the glass."

"I don't know."

I nod, and offer her my hand. She gets up without any trouble, but she avoids my eyes. I check the corners of the room for cameras. There is one, just where I thought it would be, right across from us. I take her elbow and lead her out of the room, to a place where I know we won't be observed, in the blind spot between two surveillance points.

"What?" she says irritably.

"You're Divergent," I say. I haven't been very nice to her today. Last night I saw her and her friends by the chasm, and a lapse in judgment—or sobriety—led me to lean in too close, to tell her she looked good. I'm worried that I went too far. Now I'm even more worried, but for different reasons.

She cracked the glass. She's Divergent. She's in danger.

She stares.

Then she sinks against the wall, adopting an almost-convincing aura of casualness. "What's Divergent?"

"Don't play stupid," I say. "I suspected it last time, but this time it's obvious. You manipulated the simulation; you're Divergent. I'll delete the footage, but unless you want to wind up dead at the bottom of the chasm, you'll figure out how to hide it during the simulations! Now, if you'll excuse me."

I walk back to the simulation room, pulling the door closed behind me. It's easy to delete the footage—just a few keystrokes and it's done, the record clean. I double-check her file, making sure the only thing that's in there is the data from the first simulation. I'll have to come up with a way to explain where the data from this session went. A good lie, one that Eric and Max will actually believe.

In a hurry, I take out my pocketknife and wedge it between the panels covering the motherboard of the computer, prying them apart. Then I go into the hallway, to the drinking fountain, and fill my mouth with water.

When I return to the simulation room, I spit some of the water into the gap between the panels. I put my knife away and wait.

A minute or so later, the screen goes dark. Dauntless headquarters is basically a leaky cave—water damage happens all the time.

+ + +

I was desperate.

I sent a message through the same factionless man I used as a messenger last time I wanted to get in touch with my mother. I arranged to meet her inside the last car of the ten-fifteen train from Dauntless headquarters. I assume she'll know how to find me.

I sit with my back against the wall, an arm curled around one of my knees, and watch the city pass. Night trains don't move as fast as day trains between stops. It's easier to observe how the buildings change as the train draws closer to the center of the city, how they grow taller but narrower, how pillars of glass stand next to smaller, older stone structures. Like one city layered on top of another on top of another.

Someone runs alongside the train when it reaches the north side of the city. I stand up, holding one of the railings along the wall, and Evelyn stumbles into the car wearing Amity boots, an Erudite dress, and a Dauntless jacket. Her hair is pulled back, making her already-severe face even harsher.

"Hello," she says.

"Hi," I say.

"Every time I see you, you're bigger," she says. "I guess there's no point in worrying that you're eating well."

"Could say the same to you," I say, "but for different reasons."

I know she's not eating well. She's factionless, and the Abnegation haven't been providing as much aid as they usually do, with the Erudite bearing down on them the way they are.

I reach behind me and grab the backpack I brought with cans from the Dauntless storeroom.

"It's just bland soup and vegetables, but it's better than nothing," I say when I offer it to her.

"Who says I need your help?" Evelyn says carefully. "I'm doing just fine, you know."

"Yeah, that's not for you," I say. "It's for all your skinny friends. If I were you, I wouldn't turn down food."

"I'm not," she says, taking the backpack. "I'm just not used to you caring. It's a little disarming."

"I'm familiar with the feeling," I say coldly. "How long was it before you checked in on my life? Seven years?"

Evelyn sighs. "If you asked me to come here just to start this argument again, I'm afraid I can't stay long."

"No," I say. "No, that's not why I asked you to come here."

I didn't want to contact her at all, but I knew I couldn't tell any of the Dauntless what I had learned about the Abnegation attack—I don't know how loyal to the faction and its policies they are—and I had to tell someone. The last time I spoke to Evelyn, she seemed to know things about the city that I didn't. I assumed she might know how to help me with this, before it's too late.

It's a risk, but I'm not sure where else to turn.

"I've been keeping an eye on Max," I say. "You said the Erudite were involved with the Dauntless, and you were right. They're planning something together, Max and Jeanine and who knows who else."

I tell her what I saw on Max's computer, the supply lists and the maps. I tell her what I've observed about the Erudite's attitude toward Abnegation, the reports, how they're poisoning even Dauntless minds against our former faction.

When I finish, Evelyn doesn't look surprised, or even grave. In fact, I have no idea how to read her expression. She's quiet for a few seconds, and then she says, "Did you see any indication of when this might happen?"

"No," I say.

"How about numbers? How large a force do Dauntless and Erudite intend to use? Where do they intend to summon it from?"

"I don't know," I say, frustrated. "I don't really care, either. No matter how many recruits they get, they'll mow down the Abnegation in seconds. It's not like they're trained to defend themselves—not like they would even if they knew how, either."

"I knew something was going on," Evelyn says, furrowing her brow. "The lights are on at Erudite headquarters all the time now. Which means that they're not afraid of getting in trouble with the council leaders anymore, which . . . suggests something about their growing dissent."

"Okay," I say. "How do we warn them?"

"Warn who?"

"The Abnegation!" I say hotly. "How do we warn the Abnegation that they're going to be killed, how do we warn the Dauntless that their leaders are conspiring against the council, how—"

I pause. Evelyn is standing with her hands loose at her sides, her face relaxed and passive. *Our city is changing, Tobias.* That's what she said to me when we first saw each other again. *Sometime soon, everyone will have to choose a side, and I know which one you would rather be on.*

"You already knew," I say slowly, struggling to process the truth. "You knew they were planning something like this, and have been for a while. You're waiting for it. Counting on it."

"I have no lingering affection for my former faction. I don't want them, or any faction, to continue to control this city and the people in it," Evelyn says. "If someone wants to take out my enemies for me, I'm going to let them."

"I can't believe you," I say. "They're not all Marcus, Evelyn. They're *defenseless.*"

"You think they're so innocent," she says. "You don't know them. I know them, I've *seen* them for who they really are."

Her voice is low, throaty.

"How do you think your father managed to lie to you about me all those years? You think the other Abnegation leaders didn't help him, didn't perpetuate the lie? *They* knew I wasn't pregnant, that no one had called a doctor, that there *was no body.* But they still told you I was dead, didn't they?"

It hadn't occurred to me before. There was no body. No body, but still all the men and women sitting in my father's house on that awful morning and at the funeral the following evening played the game of pretend for me, and for the rest of the Abnegation community, saying even in their silence, *No one would ever leave us. Who would want to?*

I shouldn't be so surprised to find that a faction is full of liars, but I guess there are parts of me that are still naive, still like a child.

Not anymore.

"Think about it," Evelyn said. "Are those people—the kind of people who would tell a child that his mother was dead just to save face—are they the ones you want to help? Or do you want to help remove them from power?"

I thought I knew. Those innocent Abnegation, with their constant acts of service and their deferent head-bobbing, they needed to be saved.

But those *liars*, who forced me into grief, who left me alone with the man who caused me pain—should they be saved?

I can't look at her, can't answer her. I wait for the train to pass a platform, and then jump off without looking back.

+ + +

"Don't take this the wrong way, but you look awful."

Shauna sinks into the chair next to mine, setting her tray down. I feel like yesterday's conversation with my mother was a sudden, earsplitting noise, and now every other sound is muffled. I've always known that my father was cruel. But I always thought the other Abnegation were innocent; deep down, I've always thought of myself as weak for leaving them, as a kind of traitor to my own values.

Now it seems like no matter what I decide, I'll be betraying someone. If I warn the Abnegation about the attack plans I found on Max's computer, I'll be betraying Dauntless. If I don't warn them, I betray my former faction again, in a much greater way than I did before. I have no choice but to decide, and the thought of deciding makes me feel sick.

I went through today the only way I knew how: I got up and went to work. I posted the rankings—which were a source of some contention, with me advocating for giving heavier weight to improvement, and Eric advocating for consistency. I went to eat. I put myself through the motions as if by muscle memory alone.

"You going to eat any of that?" Shauna says, nodding to my plate full of food.

I shrug. "Maybe."

I can tell she's about to ask what's wrong, so I introduce a new topic. "How's Lynn doing?"

"You would know better than I do," she says. "Getting to see her fears and all that."

I cut a piece from my hunk of meat and chew it.

"What's that like?" she asks cautiously, raising an eyebrow at me. "Seeing all their fears, I mean."

"Can't talk to you about her fears," I say. "You know that."

"Is that your rule, or Dauntless's rule?"

"Does it matter?"

Shauna sighs. "Sometimes I feel like I don't even know her, that's all."

We eat the rest of our meals without speaking. That's what I like most about Shauna: she doesn't feel the need to fill the empty spaces. When we're done, we leave the dining hall together, and Zeke calls out to us from across the Pit.

"Hey!" he says. He's spinning a roll of tape around his finger. "Want to go punch something?"

"Yes," Shauna and I say in unison.

We walk toward the training room, Shauna updating Zeke on her week at the fence—"Two days ago the idiot I was on patrol with started freaking out, swearing he saw something out there. . . . Turns out it was a *plastic bag*"—and

Zeke sliding his arm across her shoulders. I run my fingers over my knuckles and try not to get in their way.

When we get closer to the training room, I think I hear voices inside. Frowning, I push the door open with my foot. Standing inside are Lynn, Uriah, Marlene, and . . . Tris. The collision of worlds startles me a little.

"I thought I heard something in here," I say.

Uriah is firing at a target with one of the plastic pellet guns the Dauntless keep around for fun—I know for a fact that he doesn't own it, so this one must be Zeke's—and Marlene is chewing on something. She grins at me and waves when I walk in.

"Turns out it's my idiot brother," says Zeke. "You're not supposed to be here after hours. Careful, or Four will tell Eric, and then you'll be as good as scalped."

Uriah tucks the gun under his waistband, against the small of his back, without turning on the safety. He'll probably end up with a welt on his butt later from the gun firing into his pants. I don't mention it to him.

I hold the door open to usher them through it. As she passes me, Lynn says, "You wouldn't tell Eric."

"No, I wouldn't," I say. When Tris passes me I put out a hand, and it fits automatically in the space between her shoulder blades. I don't even know if that was intentional or not. And I don't really care.

The others start down the hallway, our original plan of spending time in the training room forgotten once Uriah and Zeke start bickering and Shauna and Marlene share the rest of a muffin.

"Wait a second," I say to Tris. She turns to me, looking worried, so I try to smile, but it's hard to feel like smiling right now.

I noticed tension in the training room when I posted the rankings earlier this evening—I never thought, when I was tallying up the points for the rankings, that maybe I should mark her down for her protection. It would have been an insult to her skill in the simulations to put her any lower on the list, but maybe she would have preferred the insult to the growing rift between her and her fellow transfers.

Even though she's pale and exhausted, and there are little cuts around each of her nail beds, and a wavering look in her eyes, I know that's not the case. This girl would never want to be tucked safely in the middle of the pack, never.

"You belong here, you know that?" I say. "You belong with us. It'll be over soon, so . . . just hold on, okay?"

The back of my neck suddenly feels hot, and I scratch at it with one hand, unable to meet her eyes, though I can *feel* them on me as the silence stretches.

Then she slips her fingers between mine, and I stare at her, startled. I squeeze her hand, lightly, and it registers through my turmoil and my exhaustion that though I've touched her half a dozen times—each one a lapse in judgment—this is the first time she's ever done it back.

Then she turns and runs to catch up with her friends.

And I stand in the hallway, alone, grinning like an idiot.

+ + +

I try to sleep for the better part of an hour, twisting under the covers to find a comfortable position. But it seems like someone has replaced my mattress with a bag of rocks. Or maybe it's just that my mind is too busy for sleep.

Eventually I give up, putting on my shoes and jacket and walking to the Pire, the way I do every time I can't sleep. I think about running the fear landscape program again, but I didn't think to replenish my supply of simulation serum this afternoon, and it would be a hassle to get some now. Instead I walk to the control room, where Gus greets me with a grunt and the other two on staff don't even notice me come in.

I don't try to go through Max's files again—I feel like I know everything I need to know, which is that something bad is coming and I have no idea whether I'll try to stop it.

I need to tell *someone*, I need *someone* to share in this with me, to tell me what to do. But there's no one that I would trust with something like this. Even my friends here were born and raised in Dauntless; how can I know that they wouldn't trust their leaders implicitly? I can't know.

For some reason, Tris's face comes to mind, open but stern as she clasps my hand in the hallway.

I scroll through the footage, looking over the city streets and then returning to the Dauntless compound. Most of the hallways are so dark, I couldn't see anything even if it was there. In my headphones, I hear only the rush of water in the chasm or the whistle of wind through the alleys. I sigh, leaning my head into my hand, and watch the changing images, one after another, and let them lull me into something like sleep.

"Go to bed, Four," Gus says from across the room.

I jerk awake, and nod. If I'm not actually looking at the footage it's not a good idea for me to be in the control room. I log out of my account and walk down the hallway to the elevator, blinking myself awake.

As I walk across the lobby, I hear a scream coming from below, coming from the Pit. It's not a good-natured Dauntless shout, or the shriek of someone who is scared but delighted, or anything but the particular tone, the particular pitch of terror.

Small rocks scatter behind me as I run down to the bottom of the Pit, my breathing fast and heavy, but even.

Three tall, dark-clothed people stand near the railing below. They are crowded around a fourth, smaller target, and even though I can't see much about them, I know a fight when I see one. Or, I would call it a fight, if it wasn't three against one.

One of the attackers wheels around, sees me, and sprints in the other direction. When I get closer I see one of the remaining attackers holding the target up, over the chasm, and I shout, "Hey!"

I see her hair, blond, and I can hardly see anything else. I collide with one of the attackers—Drew, I can tell by the color of his hair, orange-red—and slam him into the chasm barrier. I hit him once, twice, three times in the face, and he collapses to the ground, and then I'm kicking him and I can't think, can't think at all.

"Four." Her voice is quiet, ragged, and it's the only thing that could possibly reach me in this place. She's hanging from the railing, dangling over the chasm like a piece of bait from a fishing hook. The other one, the last attacker, is gone.

I run toward her, grabbing her under her shoulders, and pull her over the edge of the railing. I hold her against me. She presses her face to my shoulder, twisting her fingers into my shirt.

Drew is on the ground, collapsed. I hear him groan as I carry her away—not to the infirmary, where the others who went after her would think to look for her, but to my apartment, in its lonely, removed corridor. I shove my way through the apartment door and lay her down on my bed. I run my fingers over her nose and cheekbones to check for breaks, then I feel for her pulse, and lean in close to listen to her breathing. Everything seems normal, steady. Even the bump on the back of her head, though swollen and scraped, doesn't seem serious. She isn't badly injured, but she could have been.

My hands shake when I pull away from her. *She* isn't badly injured, but Drew might be. I don't even know how many times I hit him before she finally said my name and woke me up. The rest of my body starts to shake, too, and I make sure there's a pillow supporting her head, then leave the apartment to go back to the railing next to the Pit. On the way, I try to replay the last few minutes in my mind, try to recall what I punched and when and how hard, but the whole thing is lost to a dizzy fit of anger.

I wonder if this is what it was like for him, I think, remembering the wild, frantic look in Marcus's eyes every time he got angry.

When I reach the railing, Drew is still there, lying in a strange, crumpled position on the ground. I pull his arm across my shoulders and half lift, half drag him to the infirmary.

+ + +

When I make it back to my apartment, I immediately walk to the bathroom to wash the blood from my hands—a few of my knuckles are split, cut from the impact with Drew's face. If Drew was there, the other attacker had to be Peter, but who was the third? Not Molly—the shape was too tall, too big. In fact, there's only one initiate that size.

Al.

I check my reflection, like I'm going to see little pieces of Marcus staring back at me there. There's a cut at the corner of my mouth—did Drew hit me back at some point? It doesn't matter. My lapse in memory doesn't matter. What matters is that Tris is breathing.

I keep my hands under the cool water until it runs clear, then dry them on the towel and go to the freezer for an ice pack. As I carry it toward her, I realize she's awake.

"Your hands," she says, and it's a ridiculous thing to say, so stupid, to be worried about my *hands* when she was just dangled over the chasm by her throat.

"My hands," I say irritably, "are none of your concern."

I lean over her, slipping the ice pack under her head, where I felt a bump earlier. She lifts her hand and touches her fingertips lightly to my mouth.

I never thought you could feel a touch this way, like a jolt of energy. Her fingers are soft, curious.

"Tris," I say. "I'm all right."

"Why were you there?"

"I was coming back from the control room. I heard a scream."

"What did you do to them?"

"I deposited Drew at the infirmary a half hour ago. Peter and Al ran. Drew claimed they were just trying to scare you. At least, I think that's what he was trying to say."

"He's in bad shape?"

"He'll live. In what condition, I can't say," I spit.

I shouldn't let her see this side of me, the side that derives savage pleasure from Drew's pain. I shouldn't *have* this side.

She reaches for my arm, squeezes it. "Good," she says.

I look down at her. She has that side, too, she must have it. I saw the way she looked when she beat Molly, like she was going to keep going whether her opponent was unconscious or not. Maybe she and I are the same.

Her face contorts, twists, and she starts to cry. Most of the time, when someone has cried in front of me, I've felt squeezed, like I needed to escape their company in order to breathe. I don't feel that way with her. I don't worry, with her, that she expects too much from me, or that she needs anything from me at all. I sink down to the floor so we're on the same plane, and watch her carefully for a moment. Then I touch my hand to her cheek, careful not to press against any of her still-forming bruises. I run my thumb over her cheekbone. Her skin is warm.

I don't have the right word for how she looks, but even now, with parts of her face swollen and discolored, there's something striking about her, something I haven't seen before.

In that moment I'm able to accept the inevitability of how I feel, though not with joy. I need to talk to someone. I need to trust someone. And for whatever reason, I know, I *know* it's her.

I'll have to start by telling her my name.

+++

I approach Eric in the breakfast line, standing behind him with my tray as he uses a long-handled spoon to scoop scrambled eggs onto his plate.

"If I told you that one of the initiates was attacked last night by a few of the other initiates," I say, "would you even care?"

He pushes the eggs to one side of his plate, and lifts a shoulder. "I might care that their instructor doesn't seem to be able to control his initiates," Eric says as I pick up a bowl of cereal for myself. He eyes my split knuckles. "I might care that this hypothetical attack would be the *second* under that instructor's watch . . . whereas the Dauntless-borns don't seem to have this problem."

"Tensions between the transfers are naturally higher— they don't know each other, or this faction, and their backgrounds are wildly different," I say. "And you're their leader, shouldn't you be responsible for keeping them 'under control'?"

He sets a piece of toast next to his eggs with some tongs. Then he leans in close to my ear and says, "You're on thin ice, *Tobias*," he hisses. "Arguing with me in front of the others. 'Lost' simulation results. Your obvious bias toward the weaker initiates in the rankings. Even Max agrees now. If there *was* an attack, I don't think he would be too happy with you, and he might not object when I suggest that you be removed from your post."

"Then you'd be out an initiation instructor a week before the end of initiation."

"I can finish it out myself."

"I can only *imagine* what it would be like under your watch," I say, narrowing my eyes. "We wouldn't even need to make any cuts. They would all die or defect on their own."

"If you're not careful you won't have to imagine anything." He reaches the end of the food line and turns to me. "Competitive environments create tension, Four. It's natural for that tension to be released somehow." He smiles a little, stretching the skin between his piercings. "An attack would certainly show us, in a real-world situation, who the strong ones and the weak ones are, don't you think? We wouldn't have to rely on the test results at all, that way. We could make a more informed decision about who doesn't belong here. That is . . . if an attack were to happen."

The implication is clear: As the survivor of the attack, Tris would be viewed as weaker than the other initiates, and fodder for elimination. Eric wouldn't rush to the aid of the victim, but would rather advocate for her expulsion from Dauntless, as he did before Edward left of his own accord. I don't want Tris to be forced into factionlessness.

"Right," I say lightly. "Well, it's a good thing no attacks have happened recently, then."

I dump some milk on top of my cereal and walk to my table. Eric won't do anything to Peter, Drew, or Al, and I can't do anything without stepping out of line and suffering the repercussions. But maybe—maybe I don't have to do this alone. I put my tray down between Zeke and Shauna and say, "I need your help with something."

+ + +

After the fear landscape explanation is over and the initiates are dismissed for lunch, I pull Peter aside into the observation room next to the bare simulation room. It contains rows of chairs, ready for the initiates to sit in as they wait to take their final test. It also contains Zeke and Shauna.

"We need to have a chat," I say.

Zeke lurches toward Peter, slamming him against the concrete wall with alarming force. Peter cracks the back of his head, and winces.

"Hey there," Zeke says, and Shauna moves toward them, spinning a knife on her palm.

"What is this?" Peter says. He doesn't even look a little afraid, even when Shauna catches the blade by the handle and touches the point to his cheek, creating a dimple. "Trying to *scare* me?" he sneers.

"No," I say. "Trying to make a point. You're not the only one with friends who are willing to do some harm."

"I don't think initiation instructors are supposed to threaten initiates, do you?" Peter gives me a wide-eyed look, one I might mistake for innocence if I didn't know what he was really like. "I'll have to ask Eric, though, just to be sure."

"I didn't threaten you," I say. "I'm not even touching you. And according to the footage of this room that's stored on the control room computers, we're not even in here right now."

Zeke grins like he can't help it. That was his idea.

"I'm the one who's threatening you," Shauna says, almost in a growl. "One more violent outburst and I'm going to teach you a lesson about justice." She holds the knife point over his eye, and brings it down slowly, pressing the point to his eyelid. Peter freezes, barely moving even to breathe. "An eye for an eye. A bruise for a bruise."

"Eric may not care if you go after your peers," Zeke says, "but we do, and there are a lot of Dauntless like us. People who don't think you should lay a hand on your fellow faction members. People who listen to gossip, and spread it like wildfire. It won't take long for us to tell them what kind of worm you are, or for them to make your life very, very difficult. You see, in Dauntless, reputations tend to stick."

"We'll start with all your potential employers," Shauna says. "The supervisors in the control room—Zeke can take them; the leaders out by the fence—I'll get those. Tori knows everyone in the Pit—Four, you're friends with Tori, right?"

"Yes I am," I say. I move closer to Peter, and tilt my head. "You may be able to cause pain, initiate . . . but we can cause you lifelong misery."

Shauna takes the knife away from Peter's eye. "Think about it."

Zeke lets go of Peter's shirt and smooths it down, still smiling. Somehow the combination of Shauna's ferocity and Zeke's cheerfulness is just strange enough to be threatening. Zeke waves at Peter, and we all leave together.

"You want us to talk to people anyway, right?" Zeke asks me.

"Oh yeah," I say. "Definitely. Not just about Peter. Drew and Al, too."

"Maybe if he survives initiation, I'll accidentally trip him and he'll fall right into the chasm," Zeke says hopefully, making a plummeting gesture with his hand.

+++

The next morning, there's a crowd gathered by the chasm, all quiet and still, though the smell of breakfast beckons us all toward the cafeteria. I don't have to ask what they're gathered for.

This happens almost every year, I'm told. A death.

Like Amar's, sudden and awful and wasteful. A body pulled out of the chasm like a fish on a hook. Usually someone young—an accident, because of a daredevil stunt gone wrong, or maybe not an accident, a wounded mind further injured by the darkness, pressure, pain of Dauntless.

I don't know how to feel about those deaths. Guilty, maybe, for not seeing the pain myself. Sad, that some people can't find another way to escape.

I hear the name of the deceased spoken up ahead, and both emotions strike me hard.

Al. Al. Al.

My initiate—my *responsibility*, and I failed, because I've been so obsessed with catching Max and Jeanine, or with blaming everything on Eric, or with my indecision about warning the Abnegation. No—none of those things so much as this: that I distanced myself from them for my own protection, when I should have been drawing them out of the dark places here and into the lighter ones. Laughing with friends on the chasm rocks. Late-night tattoos after a game of Dare. A sea of embraces after the rankings are announced. Those are the things I could have shown him—even if it wouldn't have helped him, I should have tried.

I know one thing: after this year's initiation is done,

Eric won't need to try so hard to oust me from this position. I'm already gone.

+ + +

Al. Al. Al.

Why do all dead people become heroes in Dauntless? Why do we need them to? Maybe they're the only ones we can find in a faction of corrupt leaders, competitive peers, and cynical instructors. Dead people can be our heroes because they can't disappoint us later; they only improve over time, as we forget more and more about them.

Al was unsure and sensitive, and then jealous and violent, and then gone. Softer men than Al have lived and harder men than Al have died and there's no explanation for any of it.

But Tris wants one, craves one, I can see it in her face, a kind of hunger. Or anger. Or both. I can't imagine it's easy to like someone, hate them, and then lose them before any of those feelings are resolved. I follow her away from the chanting Dauntless because I'm arrogant enough to believe I can make her feel better.

Right. Sure. Or maybe I follow her because I'm tired of being so removed from everyone, and I'm no longer sure it's the best way to be.

"Tris," I say.

"What are you doing here?" she says bitterly. "Shouldn't you be paying your respects?"

"Shouldn't you?" I move toward her.

"Can't pay respect when you don't have any." I'm surprised, for a moment, that she can manage to be so cold—Tris isn't always nice, but she's rarely cavalier about anything. It only takes her a second to shake her head. "I didn't mean that."

"Ah."

"This is ridiculous," she says, flushing. "He throws himself off a ledge and Eric's calling it brave? Eric, who tried to have you throw knives at Al's head?" Her face contorts. "He wasn't brave! He was depressed and a coward and he almost killed me! Is that the kind of thing we respect here?"

"What do you want them to do?" I say as gently as I can—which isn't saying much. "Condemn him? Al's already dead. He can't hear it, and it's too late."

"It's not *about* Al," she says. "It's about everyone watching! Everyone who now sees hurling themselves into the chasm as a viable option. I mean, why *not* do it if everyone calls you a hero afterward? Why not do it if everyone will remember your name?" But of course, it is about Al, and she knows that. "It's . . ." She's struggling, fighting with herself. "I can't . . . This would *never* have happened in Abnegation! None of it! Never. This place warped him and ruined him, and I don't care if saying that makes me a Stiff, I don't care, I don't *care*!"

My paranoia is so deeply ingrained, I look automatically at the camera buried in the wall above the drinking fountain, disguised by the blue lamp fixed there. The people in the control room can see us, and if we're unlucky, they could choose this moment to hear us, too. I can see it now, Eric calling Tris a faction traitor, Tris's body on the pavement near the railroad tracks . . .

"Careful, Tris," I say.

"Is that all you can say?" She frowns at me. "That I should be *careful*? That's *it*?"

I understand that my response wasn't exactly what she was expecting, but for someone who just railed against Dauntless recklessness, she's definitely acting like one of them.

"You're as bad as the Candor, you know that?" I say. The Candor are always running their mouths, never thinking about the consequences. I pull her away from the drinking fountain, and then I'm close to her face and I can see her dead eyes floating in the water of the underground river and I can't stand it, not when she was just attacked and who knows what would have happened if I hadn't heard her scream.

"I'm not going to say this again, so listen carefully." I put my hands on her shoulders. "They are watching you. *You*, in particular."

I remember Eric's eyes on her after the knife throwing. His questions about her deleted simulation data. I claimed water damage. He thought it was interesting that the water damage occurred not five minutes after Tris's simulation ended. *Interesting*.

"Let go of me," she says.

I do, immediately. I don't like hearing her voice that way.

"Are they watching you, too?"

Always have been, always will be. "I keep trying to help you, but you refuse to be helped."

"Oh, right. Your help," she says. "Stabbing my ear with a knife and taunting me and yelling at me more than you yell at anyone else, it sure is helpful."

"Taunting you? You mean when I threw the knives? I wasn't taunting you!" I shake my head. "I was reminding you that if you failed, someone else would have to take your place."

To me, at the time, it almost seemed obvious. I thought, since she seemed to understand me better than most people, she might understand that, too. But of course she didn't. She's not a mind reader.

"Why?" she says.

"Because . . . you're from Abnegation," I say. "And . . . it's when you're acting selflessly that you are at your bravest. And if I were you, I would do a better job of pretending that selfless impulse is going away, because if the wrong people discover it . . . well, it won't be good for you."

"Why? Why do they care about my intentions?"

"Intentions are the only thing they care about. They try to make you think they care about what you do, but they don't. They don't want you to act a certain way, they want you to *think* a certain way. So you're easy to understand. So you won't pose a threat to them."

I put my hand on the wall near her face and lean into it, thinking of the tattoos forming a line on my back. It wasn't getting the tattoos that made me a faction traitor. It was what they meant to me—an escape from the narrow thinking of any one faction, the thinking that slices away at all the different parts of me, paring me down to just one version of myself.

"I don't understand why they care what I think, as long as I'm acting how they want me to," she says.

"You're acting how they want you to now, but what happens when your Abnegation-wired brain tells you to do something else, something they don't want?"

Much as I like him, Zeke is the perfect example.

Dauntless-born, Dauntless-raised, Dauntless-chosen. I can count on him to approach everything the same way. He was trained to from birth. To him, there are no other options.

"I might not need you to help me. Ever think about that?" she says. I want to laugh at the question. Of course she doesn't need me. When was it ever about that? "I'm not weak, you know. I can do this on my own."

"You think my first instinct is to protect you." I shift so I'm a little closer to her. "Because you're small, or a girl, or a Stiff. But you're wrong."

Even closer. I touch her chin, and for a moment I think about closing this gap completely.

"My first instinct is to push you until you break, just to see how hard I have to press," I say, and it's a strange admission, and a dangerous one. I don't mean her any harm, and never have, and I hope she knows that's not what I mean. "But I resist it."

"Why is that your first instinct?" she says.

"Fear doesn't shut you down," I say. "It wakes you up. I've seen it. It's fascinating." Her eyes in every fear simulation, ice and steel and blue flame. The short, slight girl with the wire-taut arms. A walking contradiction. My hand slips over her jaw, touches her neck. "Sometimes I just want to see it again. Want to see you awake."

Her hands touch my waist, and she pulls herself against me, or pulls me against her, I can't tell which. Her hands move over my back, and I *want* her, in a way I haven't felt before, not just some kind of mindless physical drive but a real, specific desire. Not for "someone," just for *her*.

I touch her back, her hair. It's enough, for now.

"Should I be crying?" she asks, and it takes me a second to realize she's talking about Al again. Good, because if this embrace made her want to cry, I would have to admit to knowing absolutely nothing about romance. Which might be true anyway. "Is there something wrong with me?"

"You think I know anything about tears?" Mine come without prompting and disappear a few seconds later.

"If I had forgiven him . . . do you think he would be alive now?"

"I don't know." I set my hand on her cheek, my fingers stretching back to her ear. She really is small. I don't mind it.

"I feel like it's my fault," she says.

So do I.

"It isn't your fault." I bring my forehead to hers. Her breaths are warm against my face. I was right, this is better than keeping my distance, this is much better.

"But I should have. I should have forgiven him."

"Maybe. Maybe there's more we all could have done," I say, and then I spit out an Abnegation platitude without thinking. "But we just have to let the guilt remind us to do better next time."

She pulls away immediately, and I feel that familiar impulse, to be mean to her so she forgets what I said, so she doesn't ask me any questions.

"What faction did you come from, Four?"

I think you know. "It doesn't matter. This is where I am now. Something you would do well to remember for yourself."

I don't want to be close to her anymore; it's all I want to do.

I want to kiss her; now is not the time.

I touch my lips to her forehead, and neither of us moves. No turning back now, not for me.

+ + +

Something she said sticks with me all day. *This would never have happened in Abnegation.*

At first I find myself thinking, *She just doesn't know what they're really like.*

But I'm wrong, and she's right. Al would not have died in Abnegation, and he would not have attacked her there, either. They may not be as purely good as I once believed—or wanted to believe—but they certainly aren't evil, either.

I see the map of the Abnegation sector, the one I found on Max's computer, printed on my eyelids when I close my eyes. If I warn them, if I don't, I'm a traitor either way, to one thing or another. So if loyalty is impossible, what do I strive for instead?

+ + +

It takes me a while to figure out a plan, how to go about this. If she was a normal Dauntless girl and I was a normal Dauntless boy, I would ask her on a date and we would make out by the chasm and I might show off my knowledge of Dauntless headquarters. But that feels too ordinary, after the things we've said to each other, after I've seen into the darkest parts of her mind.

Maybe that's the problem—it's all one-sided right now, because I know her, I know what she's afraid of and what she loves and what she hates, but all she knows about me is what I've told her. And what I've told her is so vague as to be negligible, because I have a problem with specificity.

After that I know what to do, it's just the doing it that's the problem.

I turn on the computer in the fear landscape room and set it to follow my program. I get two syringes of simulation serum from the storeroom, and put them in the little black box I have for this purpose. Then I set out for the transfer dormitory, not sure how I'll get her alone long enough to ask her to come with me.

But then I see her with Will and Christina, standing by the railing, and I should call her name and ask her, but I can't do it. Am I crazy, thinking of letting her into my head? Letting her see Marcus, learn my name, know everything I've tried so hard to keep hidden?

I start up the paths of the Pit again, my stomach churning. I reach the lobby, and the city lights are starting to go out all around us. I hear her footsteps on the stairs. She came after me.

I turn the black box in my hand.

"Since you're here," I say, like it's casual, which is ridiculous, "you might as well go in with me."

"Into your fear landscape?"

"Yes."

"I can do that?"

"The serum connects you to the program, but the program determines whose landscape you go through. And right now, it's set to put us through mine."

"You would let me see that?"

I can't quite look at her. "Why else do you think I'm going in?" My stomach hurts even worse. "There are some things I want to show you."

I open the box and take out the first syringe. She tilts her head, and I inject the serum, just like we always do during fear simulations. But instead of injecting myself with the other syringe, I offer her the box. This is supposed to be my way of evening things out, after all.

"I've never done this before," she says.

"Right here." I touch the place. She shakes a little as she inserts the needle, and the deep ache is familiar, but it no longer bothers me. I've done this too many times. I watch her face. No turning back, no turning back. Time to see what we're both made of.

I take her hand, or maybe she takes mine, and we walk into the fear landscape room together.

"See if you can figure out why they call me Four."

The door closes behind us, and the room is black. She moves closer to me and says, "What's your real name?"

"See if you can figure that out, too."

The simulation begins.

The room opens up to a wide blue sky, and we are on the roof of the building, surrounded by the city, sparkling in the sun. It's beautiful for just a moment before the wind starts, fierce and powerful, and I put my arm around her because I know she's steadier than I am, in this place.

I'm having trouble breathing, which is normal for me,

here. I find the rush of air suffocating, and the height makes me want to curl into a ball and hide.

"We have to jump off, right?" she says, and I remember that I can't curl into a ball and hide; I have to face this now.

I nod.

"On three, okay?"

I nod again. All I have to do is follow her, that's all I have to do.

She counts to three and drags me behind her as she runs, like she's a sailboat and I'm an anchor, pulling us both down. We fall and I struggle against the sensation with every inch of me, terror shrieking in every nerve, and then I'm on the ground, clutching my chest.

She helps me to my feet. I feel stupid, remembering how she scaled that Ferris wheel with no hesitation.

"What's next?"

I want to tell her it's not a game; my fears aren't thrilling rides she gets to go on. But she probably doesn't mean it that way.

"It's—"

The wall comes from nowhere, slamming into her back, my back, both our sides. Forcing us together, closer than we've ever been before.

"Confinement," I say, and it's worse than usual with her in here, taking up half the air. I groan a little, hunching over her. I hate it in here. I *hate* it in here.

"Hey," she says. "It's okay. Here—"

She pulls my arm around her. I've always thought of her as spare, not an ounce of extra anything on her. But her waist is soft.

"This is the first time I'm happy I'm so small," she says.

"Mmhmm."

She's talking about how to get out. Fear-landscape strategy. I am trying to focus on breathing. Then she pulls us both down, to make the box smaller, and turns so her back is against my chest, so I'm completely wrapped around her.

"This is worse," I say, because with my nervousness about the box and my nervousness about touching her combined, I can't even think straight. "This is definitely . . ."

"Shh. Arms around me."

I wrap my arms around her waist, and bury my face in her shoulder. She smells like Dauntless soap, and sweet, like apple.

I'm forgetting where I am.

She's talking about the fear landscape again, and I'm listening, but I'm also focused on how she *feels*.

"So try to forget we're here," she finishes.

"Yeah?" I put my mouth right up against her ear, on purpose this time, to keep the distraction going, but also because I get the feeling I'm not the only one who's distracted. "That easy, huh?"

"You know, most boys would enjoy being trapped in close quarters with a girl."

"Not claustrophobic people, Tris!"

"Okay, okay." She guides my hand to her chest, right under where her collarbone dips. All I can think about is what I want, which has nothing to do with getting out of this box, suddenly. "Feel my heartbeat. Can you feel it?"

"Yes."

"Feel how steady it is?"

I smile into her shoulder. "It's fast."

"Yes, well, that has nothing to do with the box." Of course it doesn't. "Every time you feel me breathe, you breathe. Focus on that."

We breathe together, once, twice.

"Why don't you tell me where this fear comes from. Maybe talking about it will help us somehow."

I feel like this fear should have vanished already, but what she's doing is keeping me at a steady level of heightened uneasiness, not taking my fear away completely. I try to focus on where this box comes from.

"Um . . . okay." *Okay, just do it, just say something real.* "This one is from my . . . fantastic childhood. Childhood punishments. The tiny closet upstairs."

Shut in the dark to think about what I did. It was better than other punishments, but sometimes I was in there for too long, desperate for fresh air.

"My mother kept our winter coats in our closet," she says, and it's a silly thing to say after what I just told her, but I can tell she doesn't know what else to do.

"I don't really want to talk about it anymore," I say with a gasp. She doesn't know what to say because no one could possibly know what to say, because my childhood pain is too pathetic for anyone else to handle—my heart rate spikes again.

"Okay. Then . . . I can talk. Ask me something."

I lift my head. It was working before, focusing on her. Her racing heart, her body against mine. Two strong skeletons wrapped in muscle, tangled together; two Abnegation transfers working on leaving tentative flirtation behind. "Why is your heart racing, Tris?"

"Well, I . . . I barely know you." I can picture her scowling. "I barely know you and I'm crammed up against you in a box, Four, what do you think?"

"If we were in your fear landscape . . ." I say. "Would I be in it?"

"I'm not afraid of you."

"Of course you're not. That's not what I meant." I meant not *Are you afraid of me?* but *Am I important enough to you to feature in the landscape anyway?*

Probably not. She's right, she hardly knows me. But still: Her heart is racing.

I laugh, and the walls break as if my laugh shook them and broke them, and the air opens up around us. I swallow a deep breath of it, and we peel away from each other. She looks at me, suspicious.

"Maybe you were cut out for Candor, because you're a terrible liar," I say.

"I think my aptitude test ruled that one out pretty well."

"The aptitude test tells you nothing."

"What are you trying to tell me? Your test isn't the reason you ended up Dauntless?"

I shrug. "Not exactly, no. I . . ."

I see something out of the corner of my eye, and turn to face it. A plain-faced, forgettable woman stands alone at the other end of the room. Between her and us is a table with a gun on it.

"You have to kill her," Tris says.

"Every time."

"She isn't real."

"She looks real. It feels real."

"If she was real, she would have killed *you* already."

"It's okay. I'll just . . . do it." I start toward the table. "This one's not so bad. Not as much panic involved."

Panic and terror aren't the only kinds of fear. There are deeper kinds, more terrible kinds. Apprehension and heavy, heavy dread.

I load the gun without thinking about it, hold it out in front of me, and look at her face. She's blank, like she knows what I'm going to do and accepts it.

She's not dressed in the clothes of any faction, but she might as well be Abnegation, standing there waiting for me to hurt her, the way they would. The way they will, if Max and Jeanine and Evelyn all get their way.

I close one eye, to focus on my target, and fire.

She falls, and I think of punching Drew until he was almost unconscious.

Tris's hand closes around my arm. "Come on. Keep moving."

We walk past the table, and I shudder with fear. Waiting for this last obstacle might be a fear in itself.

"Here we go," I say.

Creeping into the circle of light we now occupy is a dark figure, pacing so just the edge of his shoe is visible. Then he steps toward us, Marcus with his black-pit eyes and his gray clothes and his close-cut hair, showing off the contours of his skull.

"Marcus," she whispers.

I watch him. Waiting for the first blow to fall. "Here's

the part where you figure out my name."

"Is he . . ." She knows, now. She'll know forever; I can't make her forget it if I wanted to. "Tobias."

It's been so long since someone said my name that way, like it was a revelation and not a threat.

Marcus unwinds a belt from his fist.

"This is for your own good," he says, and I want to scream.

He multiplies immediately, surrounding us, the belts dragging on white tile. I curl into myself, hunching my back, waiting, waiting. The belt pulls back and I flinch before it hits, but then it doesn't.

Tris stands in front of me, her arm up, tense from head to toe. She grits her teeth as the belt wraps around her arm, and then she pulls it free, and lashes out. The movement is so powerful I'm amazed by how strong it looks, by how *hard* the belt slaps Marcus's skin.

He lunges at Tris, and I step in front of her. I'm ready this time, ready to fight back.

But the moment never comes. The lights lift and the fear landscape is over.

"That's it?" she says as I watch the place where Marcus stood. "Those were your worst fears? Why do you only have four . . . oh."

She looks at me.

"That's why they call you . . ."

I was afraid that if she knew about Marcus, she would look at me with pity, and she would make me feel weak, and small, and empty.

But she saw Marcus and she looked at *him*, with anger and without fear. She made me feel, not weak, but powerful. Strong enough to fight back.

I tug her toward me by her elbow, and kiss her cheek, slowly, letting her skin burn into mine. I hold her tightly, slouching into her.

"Hey." She sighs. "We got through it."

I put my fingers through her hair.

"You got me through it," I say.

+++

I take her to the rocks that Zeke, Shauna, and I go to sometimes, late at night. Tris and I sit on a flat stone suspended over the water, and the spray soaks my shoes, but it's not so cold that I mind. Like all initiates, she's too focused on the aptitude test, and I'm struggling with talking to her about it. I thought that when I spilled one secret, the rest would come tumbling after, but openness is a habit you form over time, and not a switch you flip whenever you want to, I'm finding.

"These are things I don't tell people, you know. Not

even my friends." I watch the dark, murky water and the things it carries—pieces of trash, discarded clothing, floating bottles like small boats setting out on a journey. "My result was as expected. Abnegation."

"Oh." She frowns. "But you chose Dauntless anyway?"

"Out of necessity."

"Why did you have to leave?"

I look away, not sure I can give voice to my reasons, because admitting them makes me a faction traitor, makes me feel like a coward.

"You had to get away from your dad," she says. "Is that why you don't want to be a Dauntless leader? Because if you were, you might have to see him again?"

I shrug. "That, and I've always felt that I don't quite belong among the Dauntless. Not the way they are now, anyway." It's not quite the truth. I'm not sure this is the moment to tell her what I know about Max and Jeanine and the attack—selfishly, I want to keep this moment to myself, just for a little while.

"But... you're incredible," she says. I raise my eyebrows at her. She seems embarrassed. "I mean, by Dauntless standards. Four fears is unheard of. How could you not belong here?"

I shrug again. The more time goes by, the stranger I find it that my fear landscape isn't riddled with fears like everyone else's. A lot of things make me nervous, anxious, uncomfortable . . . but when confronted with those things, I can *act*, I'm never paralyzed. My four fears, if I'm not careful, will paralyze me. That's the only difference.

"I have a theory that selflessness and bravery aren't all that different." I look up at the Pit, rising high above us. From here I can see just a small slice of night sky. "All your life you've been training to forget yourself, so when you're in danger, it becomes your first instinct. I could belong in Abnegation just as easily."

"Yeah, well. I left Abnegation because I wasn't selfless enough, no matter how hard I tried to be."

"That's not entirely true," I say with a smile. "That girl who let someone throw knives at her to spare a friend, who hit my dad with a belt to protect me—that selfless girl, that's not you?"

In this light, she looks like she comes from another world, her eyes rendered so pale they almost seem to glow in the dark.

"You've been paying close attention, haven't you?" she asks, like she just read my mind. But she's not talking about me looking at her face.

"I like to observe people," I say slyly.

"Maybe you were cut out for Candor, Four, because you're a terrible liar."

I set my hand down next to hers and lean closer. "Fine." Her long, narrow nose is no longer swollen from the attack, and neither is her mouth. She has a nice mouth. "I watched you because I like you. And . . . don't call me 'Four,' okay? It's . . . nice. To hear my name again."

She looks momentarily bewildered.

"But you're older than I am . . . Tobias."

It sounds so good when she says it. Like it's nothing to be ashamed of.

"Yes, that whopping two-year gap really is *insurmountable*, isn't it?"

"I'm not trying to be self-deprecating," she says stubbornly. "I just don't get it. I'm younger. I'm not pretty. I—"

I laugh, and kiss her temple.

"Don't pretend," she says, sounding a little breathless. "You know I'm not. I'm not ugly, but I am certainly not pretty."

The word "pretty," and all that it represents, seems so completely useless right now that I have no patience for it.

"Fine. You're not pretty. So?" I move my lips to her cheek, trying to work up some courage. "I like how you look." I pull back. "You're deadly smart. You're brave. And even though you found out about Marcus . . . you aren't giving me that look. Like I'm . . . a kicked puppy, or something."

"Well," she says factually. "You're not."

My instincts were right: She is worth trusting. With my secrets, with my shame, with the name that I abandoned. With the beautiful truths and the awful ones. I know it.

I touch my lips to hers. Our eyes meet, and I grin, and kiss her again, this time more sure of it.

It's not enough. I pull her closer, kiss her harder. She comes alive, putting her arms around me and leaning into me and it's still not enough, how can it be?

+ + +

I walk her back to the transfer dormitory, my shoes still damp from the river spray, and she smiles at me as she slips through the doorway. I start toward my apartment, and it doesn't take long for the giddy relief to give way to uneasiness again. Somewhere between watching that belt curl around her arm in my fear landscape and telling her that selflessness and bravery were often the same thing, I made a decision.

I turn at the next corner, not toward my apartment but toward a stairway that leads outside, right next to Max's place. I slow down when I pass his door, afraid that my footsteps will be loud enough to rouse him. Irrational.

My heart pounds when I reach the top of the stairs. A train is just passing, its silver side catching moonlight. I walk beneath the tracks and set out toward the Abnegation sector.

+ + +

Tris came from Abnegation—part of her innate power comes from them, whenever she's called upon to defend people who are weaker than she is. And I can't stand to think of the men and women who are like her falling to Dauntless-Erudite weapons. They may have lied to me, and maybe I failed them when I chose Dauntless, and maybe I'm failing Dauntless now, but I don't have to fail myself. And *I*, no matter what faction I'm in, know the right thing to do.

The Abnegation sector is so clean, not a scrap of trash on the streets, sidewalks, or lawns. The identical gray buildings are worn in places from where selfless people have refused to mend them when the factionless sector so badly needs the materials, but neat and unremarkable. The streets here could easily be a maze, but I haven't been gone long enough to forget the way to Marcus's house.

Strange, how quickly it became *his* house instead of mine, in my mind.

Maybe I don't have to tell him; I could tell another Abnegation leader, but he's the most influential one, and there's still a part of him that's my father, that tried to protect me because I'm Divergent. I try to remember the swell of power I felt in my fear landscape, when Tris showed me he was just a man, not a monster, and that I could face him. But she's not here with me now, and I feel flimsy, like I'm made of paper.

I walk up the path to the house, and my legs are rigid, like they don't have joints. I don't knock; I don't want to wake anyone else. I reach under the doormat for the spare key and unlock the front door.

It's late, but the light is still on in the kitchen. By the time I walk through the door, he's already standing where I can see him. Behind him, the kitchen table is covered with papers. He's not wearing his shoes—they're on the living room carpet, their laces undone—and his eyes are just as shadowed as they are in my nightmares about him.

"What are you doing here?" He looks me up and down. I wonder what he's looking at until I remember that I'm wearing Dauntless black, heavy boots and a jacket, tattoo ink on my neck. He comes a little closer, and I notice that I'm as tall as he is, and stronger than I ever have been.

He could never overpower me now.

"You're no longer welcome in this house," he says.

"I . . ." I stand up straighter, and not because he hates

bad posture. "I don't care," I say, and his eyebrows pop up like I just surprised him.

Maybe I did.

"I came to warn you," I say. "I found something. Attack plans. Max and Jeanine are going to attack Abnegation. I don't know when, or how."

He watches me for a second, in a way that makes me feel like I'm being measured, and then his expression shifts into a sneer.

"Max and Jeanine are going to attack," he says. "Just the two of them, armed with some simulation syringes?" His eyes narrow. "Did Max send you here? Have you become his Dauntless lackey? What, does he want to scare me?"

When I thought about warning the Abnegation, I was sure the hardest part would be getting myself through this door. It never occurred to me that he wouldn't *believe* me.

"Don't be stupid," I say. I would never have said that to him when I lived in this house, but two years of intentionally adopting Dauntless speech patterns make it come out of my mouth naturally. "If you're suspicious of Max, it's for a reason, and I'm telling you it's a good one. You're right to be suspicious. You're in danger—you all are."

"You dare to come to my house after you betrayed your

faction," he says, his voice low, "after you betrayed your *family* . . . and insult me?" He shakes his head. "I refuse to be intimidated into doing what Max and Jeanine want, and certainly not by my son."

"You know what?" I say. "Forget it. I should have gone to someone else."

I turn toward the door, and he says, "Don't walk away from me."

His hand closes around my arm, tightly. I stare at it, for a second feeling dizzy, like I'm outside of my own body, already separating myself from the moment so I can survive it.

You can fight him, I think, as I remember Tris drawing back the belt in my fear landscape to strike him.

I pull my arm free, and I'm too strong for him to hold on to. But I can only muster the strength to walk away, and he doesn't dare shout after me, not when the neighbors could hear. My hands shake a little bit, so I put them in my pockets. I don't hear the front door shut behind me, so I know he's watching me go.

It wasn't the triumphant return I pictured.

+ + +

I feel guilty when I pass through the doorway to the Pire, like there are Dauntless eyes all over me, judging me for what I just did. I went against the Dauntless leaders, and for what? For a man I hate, who didn't even believe me? It doesn't feel like it was worth it, worth being called a faction traitor.

I look through the glass floor to the chasm far beneath me, the water calm and dark, too far away to reflect any moonlight. A few hours ago I was standing right here, about to show a girl I hardly knew all the secrets I've fought so hard to protect.

She was equal to my trust, even if Marcus wasn't. *She*, and her mother, and the rest of the faction she believes in, are still worth protecting. So that's what I'm going to do.

READ ON FOR MORE EXCLUSIVE
SCENES FROM

TOLD FROM TOBIAS'S
PERSPECTIVE!

"FIRST JUMPER—TRIS!"

"CAREFUL, TRIS."

"YOU LOOK GOOD, TRIS."

"FIRST JUMPER—TRIS!"

I CHECK MY watch. The first initiate should be jumping any minute now.

The net waits beside me, wide and sturdy and lit from above by the sun. The last time I was here was last year's Choosing Day, and before then, the day I jumped. I didn't want to remember the feeling of inching toward the edge of the building, my mind and my body going haywire with terror, the awful drop, the helpless flailing of limbs, the slap of the net fibers against my arms and neck.

"How'd the prank go?" Lauren says.

It takes me a second to figure out what she means: the program, and my supposed desire to prank Zeke. "Haven't done it yet. Our work time didn't overlap much today."

"You know, if you were up for some serious studying, we could use you in tech services," she says.

"If you're recruiting, you should talk to Zeke. He's much better than I am."

"Yeah, but Zeke doesn't know when to shut it," she says. "We don't recruit for skill so much as compatibility. We spend a lot of time together."

I grin. Zeke does like to surround himself with chatter, but that's never bothered me. Sometimes it's nice not to worry about providing any conversation.

Lauren plays with one of the rings in her eyebrow, and we wait. I try to crane my neck to see the top of the building from the ground, but all I can see is sky.

"Bet you it's one of my Dauntless-borns," she says.

"It's always a Dauntless-born. No bet."

They have an unfair advantage, the Dauntless-born. They usually know what's at the bottom of the jump, though we try to keep it from them as much as possible—the only time we use this entrance to headquarters is on Choosing Day, but the Dauntless are curious, they explore the compound when they think no one is watching. They also grow up cultivating in themselves the desire to make bold moves, to take drastic action, to commit themselves fully to whatever they decide to do. It would take a strange kind of transfer to know how to do that without having been taught.

Then I see her.

Not a black streak like I was expecting, but gray, tumbling through the air. I hear a *snap* of the net pulling taught around the metal supports, and it shifts to cradle her. For a second I stare, amazed, at the familiar clothing that she wears. Then I put my hand out, into the net, so she can reach it.

She wraps her fingers around mine, and I pull her across. As she tumbles over the side, I grab her arms to steady her. She's small, and thin—fragile-looking, like the impact with the net should have shattered her. Her eyes are wide and bright blue.

"Thank you," she says. She may look fragile, but her voice is steady.

"Can't believe it," Lauren says, with more Dauntless swagger than usual. "A Stiff, the first to jump? Unheard of."

She's right. It is unheard of. It's unheard of for a Stiff to join Dauntless, even. There were no Abnegation transfers last year. And before that, for a long time, there was only me.

"There's a reason why she left them, Lauren," I say,

feeling distant from the moment, from my own body. I pull myself back and say to the initiate, "What's your name?"

"Um . . ." She hesitates, and I feel, for a strange, brief moment, like I know her. Not from my time in Abnegation, not from school, but on a deeper level, somehow, her eyes and her mouth searching for a name, dissatisfied with the one she finds, just like I was. My initiation instructor gave me an escape from my old identity. I can give her one, too.

"Think about it," I say, smiling a little. "You don't get to pick again."

"Tris," she says, like she's already sure of it.

"Tris," Lauren says. "Make the announcement, Four."

She's my initiate, after all, this transfer from Abnegation.

I look over my shoulder, at the crowd of Dauntless members who have gathered to watch the initiates jump, and I announce, "First jumper—Tris!"

This way, they'll remember her, not for the gray she wears but for her first act of bravery. Or insanity. Sometimes they're the same thing.

Everyone cheers, and as the sound fills the cavern, another initiate plummets into the net with a blood-curdling scream. A girl dressed in Candor black and white. This time, Lauren is the one to reach across the net to help her. I touch a hand to Tris's back to guide her toward the stairs, in case she's not as steady as she seems. Before she takes the first step, I say, "Welcome to Dauntless."

"CAREFUL, TRIS."

ONE ABNEGATION, FIVE Candor, two Erudite. Those are my initiates.

I'm told that Candor and Dauntless have a fairly high mutual transfer rate—we usually lose as many to them as we gain. I consider it my job to get these eight initiates through at least the first round of cuts. Last year, when Eric and Max insisted on the cuts, I fought them as hard as I dared. But it seems the cuts are here to stay, all for the sake of the Dauntless Max and Eric want to create—a faction of mindless brutality.

But I intend to leave Dauntless as soon as I find out what Max and Jeanine are up to, and if that's in the middle of initiation, so much the better.

Once all the Dauntless-borns—including Uriah, Lynn,

and Marlene—are with us, I start down the tunnel, beckoning them to follow with one hand. We walk down the dark hallway toward the Pit doors.

"This is where we divide," Lauren says, when she reaches the doors. "The Dauntless-born initiates are with me. I assume *you* don't need a tour of the place."

She smiles, and the Dauntless-borns follow her down the hallway that bypasses the Pit, leading them right into the cafeteria. I watch them leave, and once they've disappeared, I straighten up. I learned last year that in order for them to take me seriously from the beginning, I have to be hard on them from the beginning. I don't have Amar's natural charm, which won people's loyalty with just a smile or a joke, so I have to compensate in other ways.

"Most of the time I work in the control room, but for the next few weeks, I'm your instructor," I say. "My name is Four."

One of the Candor girls—tall, with dark skin and an energetic voice—speaks up. "Four? Like the number?"

I sense the beginnings of an uprising. People who don't know what my name means often like to laugh at it, and I don't like to be laughed at, especially not by a group of initiates fresh from Choosing, who have no idea what they're in for.

"Yes," I say testily. "Is there a problem?"

"No," the girl says.

"Good. We're about to go into the Pit, which you will someday learn to love. It—"

The Candor girl interrupts again. "The Pit? Clever name."

I feel a swell of irritation, and I move toward her without really deciding to. I can't have someone cracking jokes about everything I say, especially not at the beginning of initiation, when everyone's attitudes are so malleable. I have to show them all that I'm not someone to be messed with, and I have to do it now.

I lean in close to her face and stare at her for a few seconds, until I see her smile falter.

"What's your name?" I say, keeping my voice quiet.

"Christina," she says.

"Well, Christina, if I wanted to put up with Candor smart-mouths, I would have joined their faction," I say. "The first lesson you will learn from me is to keep your mouth shut. Got that?"

She nods. I turn away, my heart throbbing in my ears. I think that did it, but I can't be sure, not until initiation really begins. I push through the double doors that open up to the Pit, and for a moment, I see it like it's for the first time, the impossibly huge space, bustling with life and energy, the pulse of water in the chasm, crashing against the rocks, the echoes of conversation everywhere. Most of the time I avoid it because it's so busy, but today I love it. I can't help it.

"If you follow me," I say. "I'll show you the chasm."

+ + +

The Abnegation transfer sits at my table. For a moment I wonder if she knows who I am, or if she's somehow magnetized to me by an invisible force of Stiff that I can't help but give off. But she doesn't look at me like she knows me. And she doesn't know what a hamburger is.

"You've never had a hamburger before?" Christina says. Incredulous. The Candor are like that, amazed that not everyone lives the way that they do. It's one of the reasons I don't like them. It's like the rest of the world doesn't exist to them, but for the Abnegation, the rest of the world is all that exists, and it is full of need.

"No," Tris says. For someone so small, she has a low voice. It always sounds serious, no matter what she says. "Is that what it's called?"

"Stiffs eat plain food," I say, trying out the slang. It feels unnatural, applied to Tris; I feel like I owe her the courtesies I would owe any woman in my former faction, deferential, averted eyes and polite conversation. I have to push myself to remember that I'm not in Abnegation anymore. And neither is she.

"Why?" Christina says.

"Extravagance is considered self-indulgent and un-necessary." She says it like she's reciting it from memory. Maybe she is.

"No wonder you left."

"Yeah." Tris rolls her eyes, which surprises me. "It was just because of the food."

I try not to smile. I'm not sure it works.

Then Eric walks in, and everything goes quiet.

Eric's appointment to Dauntless leader was met with confusion and, in some cases, anger. There had never been a leader so young before, and plenty of people spoke out against the decision, voiced concerns about his youth and his Erudite background. Max made sure to silence those concerns. And so did Eric. Someone would be out-spoken one day and silent, frightened the next, almost like he had threatened them. Knowing Eric, he probably did, with soft-spoken words that twisted together into malice, clever and calculated as always.

"Who's that?" Christina says.

"His name is Eric," I say. "He's a Dauntless leader."

"Seriously? But he's so young."

I set my jaw. "Age doesn't matter here." *Connections to Jeanine Matthews do.*

He comes toward us and drops into the seat next to me. I stare at my food.

"Well, aren't you going to introduce me?" he says lightly. Like we're friends.

"This is Tris and Christina," I say.

"Ooh, a Stiff," says Eric, smirking. I worry, for a moment, that he's about to tell her where *I* came from, and I curl a hand around my knee, clenching so I don't lash out and smack him. But all he says is, "We'll see how long you last."

I still want to smack him. Or remind him that the last transfer we had from Abnegation, who is sitting right next to him, managed to knock out one of his teeth, so who knows what this next one will do. But with these new practices in place—fighting until an opponent can't stand, cuts after just a week of combat training—he's right, it's unlikely that she'll last very long, small as she is. I don't like it, but there it is.

"What have you been doing lately, Four?" Eric says.

I feel a prickle of fear, worried, for a moment, that he

knows that I'm spying on him and Max. I shrug. "Nothing, really."

"Max tells me he keeps trying to meet with you, and you don't show up," Eric says. "He requested that I find out what's going on with you."

I find it easy to discard Max's messages, like they're bits of garbage blown toward me by the wind. The backlash from Eric's appointment as Dauntless leader may not bother Eric anymore, but it still bothers Max, who has never liked his protégé as much as he was supposed to. He liked me, though I'm not sure why, since I hole up alone while the other Dauntless pull together.

"Tell him I'm satisfied with the position I currently hold," I say.

"So he wants to give you a job."

There's that suspicious probing again, oozing from his mouth like pus from a new piercing.

"So it would seem."

"And you aren't interested."

"I haven't been interested for two years."

"Well. Let's hope he gets the point, then."

He hits my shoulder, like he means it to be casual, but the force of it almost pushes me into the table. I glare at him as he walks away—I don't like to be pushed around, especially not by scrawny Erudite-lovers.

"Are you two . . . friends?" Tris asks.

"We were in the same initiate class." I decide to make a preemptive strike, to poison them against Eric before he poisons them against me. "He transferred from Erudite."

Christina raises her eyebrows, but Tris disregards the word "erudite," disregards the suspicion that ought to be written into her very skin after a lifetime in Abnegation, and says, "Were you a transfer too?"

"I thought I would only have trouble with the Candor asking too many questions," I say. "Now I've got Stiffs, too?"

As it was with Christina before, my sharpness is intended to slam doors before they open too much. But Tris's mouth twists like she tastes something sour, and she says, "It must be because you're so approachable. You know. Like a bed of nails."

Her face flushes as I stare at her, but she doesn't look away. Something about her seems familiar to me, though I swear I would remember if I had ever met such a sharp Abnegation girl, even for just a second.

"Careful, Tris," I say. Careful what you say to me, is what I mean, careful what you say to anyone, in this faction that values all the wrong things, that doesn't understand that when you come from Abnegation, standing up for your-self, even in small moments, is the height of bravery.

As I say her name, I realize how I know her. She's Andrew Prior's daughter. Beatrice. Tris.

"YOU LOOK GOOD, TRIS."

I'M NOT SURE I remember what made me laugh, but Zeke said it, and it was hilarious. Around me, the Pit sways like I'm standing on a swing. I hold the railing to steady myself and tip the rest of whatever it is I'm drinking down my throat.

Abnegation attack? What Abnegation attack? I hardly remember.

Well, that's actually a lie, but it's never too late to get comfortable with lying to yourself.

I see a blond head bobbing in the crowd and follow it down to Tris's face. For once, she's not wearing multiple layers of clothing, and her shirt collar isn't pressed right up against the bottom of her throat. I can see her shape—
Stop it, a voice in my head scolds me, before the thought can go any further.

"Tris!" The word is out of my mouth, no stopping it, don't even care to try. I walk toward her, ignoring the stares of Will, Al, and Christina. It's easy to do—her eyes seem brighter, more piercing than before.

"You look . . . different," I say. I mean to say "older," but I don't want to suggest that she looked young before. She may not bend in all the places that older women do, but no one could look at her face and see a child. No child has that ferocity.

"So do you," she says. "What are you doing?"

Drinking, I think, but she's probably noticed that.

"Flirting with death," I say, laughing. "Drinking near the chasm. Probably not a good idea."

"No, it isn't." She's not laughing. She looks wary. Wary of what, of me?

"Didn't know you had a tattoo," I say, scanning her collarbone. There are three black birds there—simple, but they almost look like they're flying across her skin. "Right. The *crows.*"

I want to ask her why she would get one of her worst fears tattooed on her body, why she would want to wear the mark of her fear forever instead of burying it, ashamed. Maybe she's not ashamed of her fears the way I'm ashamed of mine.

I look back at Zeke and Shauna, who are standing with

shoulders touching at the railing.

"I'd ask you to hang out with us," I say, "but you're not supposed to see me this way."

"What way?" she says. "Drunk?"

"Yeah . . . well, no." Suddenly it doesn't seem that funny to me. "Real, I guess."

"I'll pretend I didn't."

"Nice of you." I lean in, closer than I mean to, and I can smell her hair, feel the cool, smooth, delicate skin of her cheek against mine. I would be embarrassed that I'm acting so foolish, so forward, if she had, even for a second, pulled away. But she doesn't—if anything, she moves a little closer. "You look good, Tris," I say, because I'm not sure she knows it, and she should.

This time she laughs.

"Do me a favor and stay away from the chasm, okay?"

"Of course."

She smiles. And I wonder, for the first time, if she likes me. If she can still grin at me when I'm like this . . . well, she might.

One thing I know: For helping me forget how awful the world is, I prefer her to alcohol.

ACKNOWLEDGMENTS

Thank you, thank you, thank you to:

My husband, family (Roth-Rydz-Rosses, Fitches, Krausses, Paquettes, Johnsons, and everyone in between), and friends (writers and non-writers alike, far and wide), for your constant support, generosity, and forgiveness, without which I would surely perish. No, seriously.

Joanna Volpe, friendgent, for unfailing kindness and wisdom and All the (Good) Things. Katherine Tegen, frienditor, for all kinds of editorial wisdom and hard, hard work. The whole team at HarperCollins, for continued awesomeness for all varieties: Joel Tippie, Amy Ryan, Barb Fitzsimmons, Brenna Franzitta, Josh Weiss, Mark Rifkin, Valerie Shea, Christine Cox, Joan Giurdanella, Lauren Flower, Alison Lisnow, Sandee Roston, Diane Naughton, Colleen O'Connell, Aubry Parks-Fried, Margot Wood, Patty Rosati, Molly Thomas, Onalee Smith, Andrea Pappenheimer, Kerry Moynagh, Kathy Faber, Liz Frew, Heather Doss, Jenny Sheridan, Fran Olson, Deb Murphy, Jessica Abel, Samantha Hagerbaumer, Andrea Rosen, David Wolfson, Jean McGinley, Alpha Wong, Sheala Howley, Ruiko Tokunaga, Caitlin Garing, Beth Ives, Katie Bignell, Karen Dziekonski, Sean McManus, Randy Rosema, Pam Moore, Rosanne Romanello, Melinda

Weigel, Gwen Morton, Lillian Sun, Rosanne Lauer, Erica Ferguson, and of course, Kate Jackson, Susan Katz, and Brian Murray. I could not have a better publishing home.

Danielle Barthel, for your patient mind and special encouragement with regard to these stories in particular. Pouya Shahbazian, for showing me how to be steady even in a storm (I'm working on it). Everyone at New Leaf Literary for working so damn hard and making that work so good. Steve Younger, for humor and legal prowess in equal measure.

And last but definitely, definitely not least: all the Divergent readers (Initiates!) across the globe. Your enthusiasm for these characters made me excited to sit down with these stories and propelled me through the hard parts.

I feel like it's only fitting to end with a

‹4